DUGOUT

ADAM BEECHEN MANNY BELLO

Dugout
by Adam Beechen and Manny Bello

published by
Larry Young and Mimi Rosenheim
AiT/Planet Lar, LLC
2034 47th Avenue
San Francisco, CA 94116

First Edition: July 2008

10 9 8 7 6 5 4 3 2 1

Cover Art by Manny Bello
Book Design and Production by Whiskey Island
Lettered in the *Cheese and Crackers* font produced by Comicraft

ISBN-10: 1-932051-54-6
ISBN-13: 978-1-932051-54-4

Printed and bound in Canada by Imprimerie Lebonfon, Inc.

DUGOUT

ADAM BEECHEN MANNY BELLO

SAN FRANCISCO

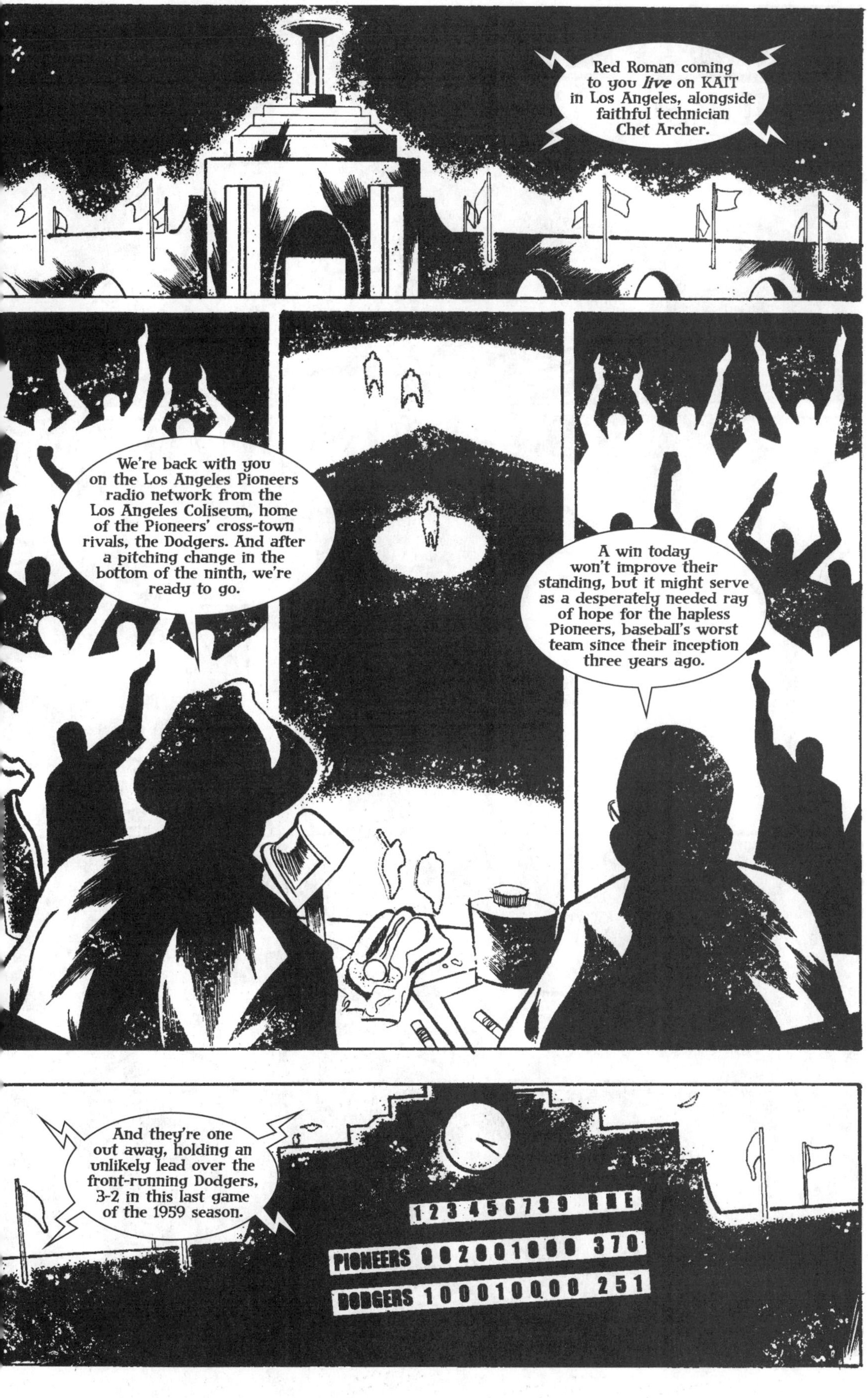

Red Roman coming to you *live* on KAIT in Los Angeles, alongside faithful technician Chet Archer.
We're back with you on the Los Angeles Pioneers radio network from the Los Angeles Coliseum, home of the Pioneers' cross-town rivals, the Dodgers. And after a pitching change in the bottom of the ninth, we're ready to go.
A win today won't improve their standing, but it might serve as a desperately needed ray of hope for the hapless Pioneers, baseball's worst team since their inception three years ago.
And they're one out away, holding an unlikely lead over the front-running Dodgers, 3-2 in this last game of the 1959 season.
123456789 RHE
PIONEERS 002001000 370
DODGERS 100010000 251

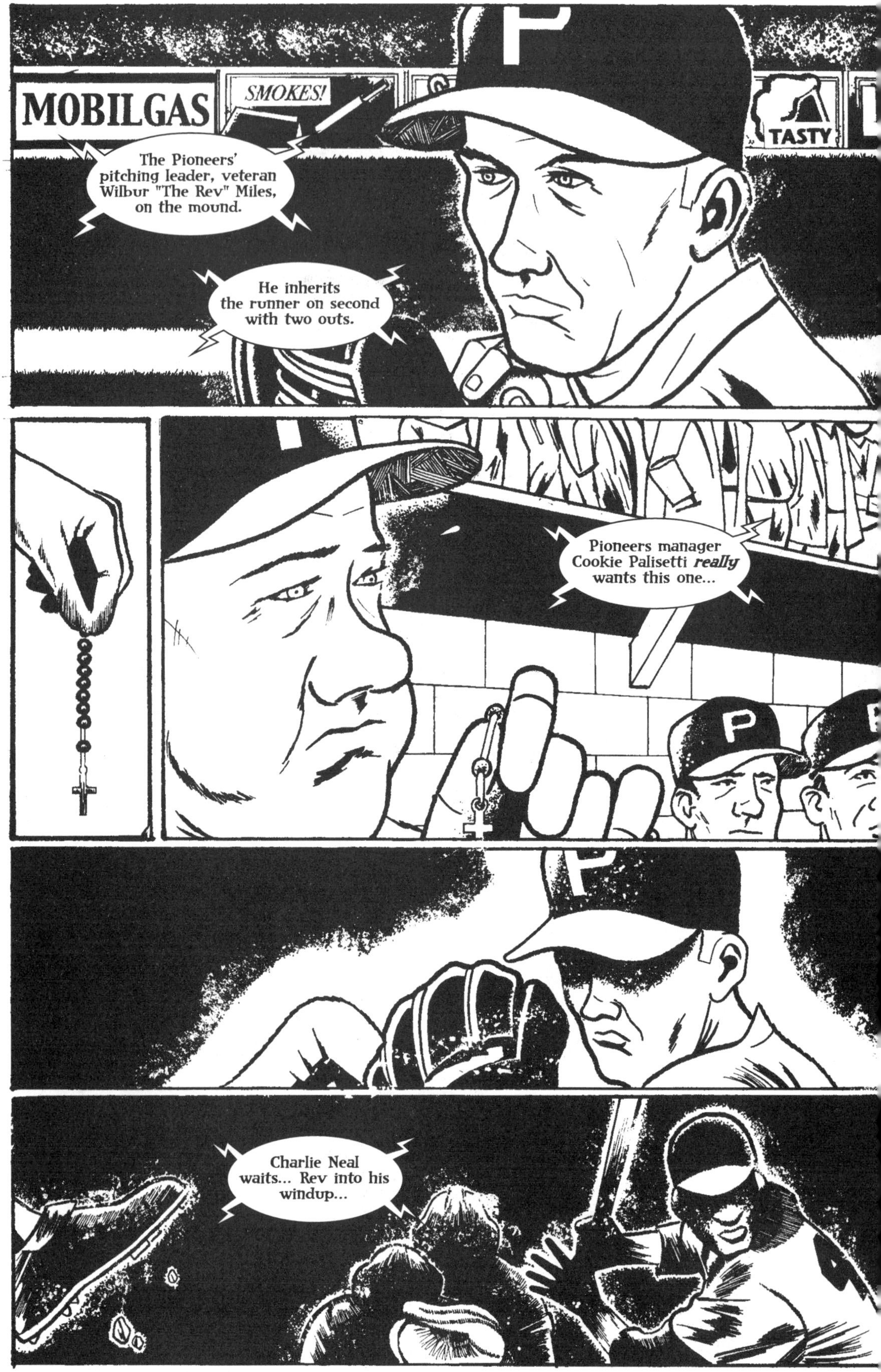
MOBILGAS
SMOKES!
TASTY
The Pioneers' pitching leader, veteran Wilbur "The Rev" Miles, on the mound.
He inherits the runner on second with two outs.
Pioneers manager Cookie Palisetti *really* wants this one...
Charlie Neal waits... Rev into his windup...

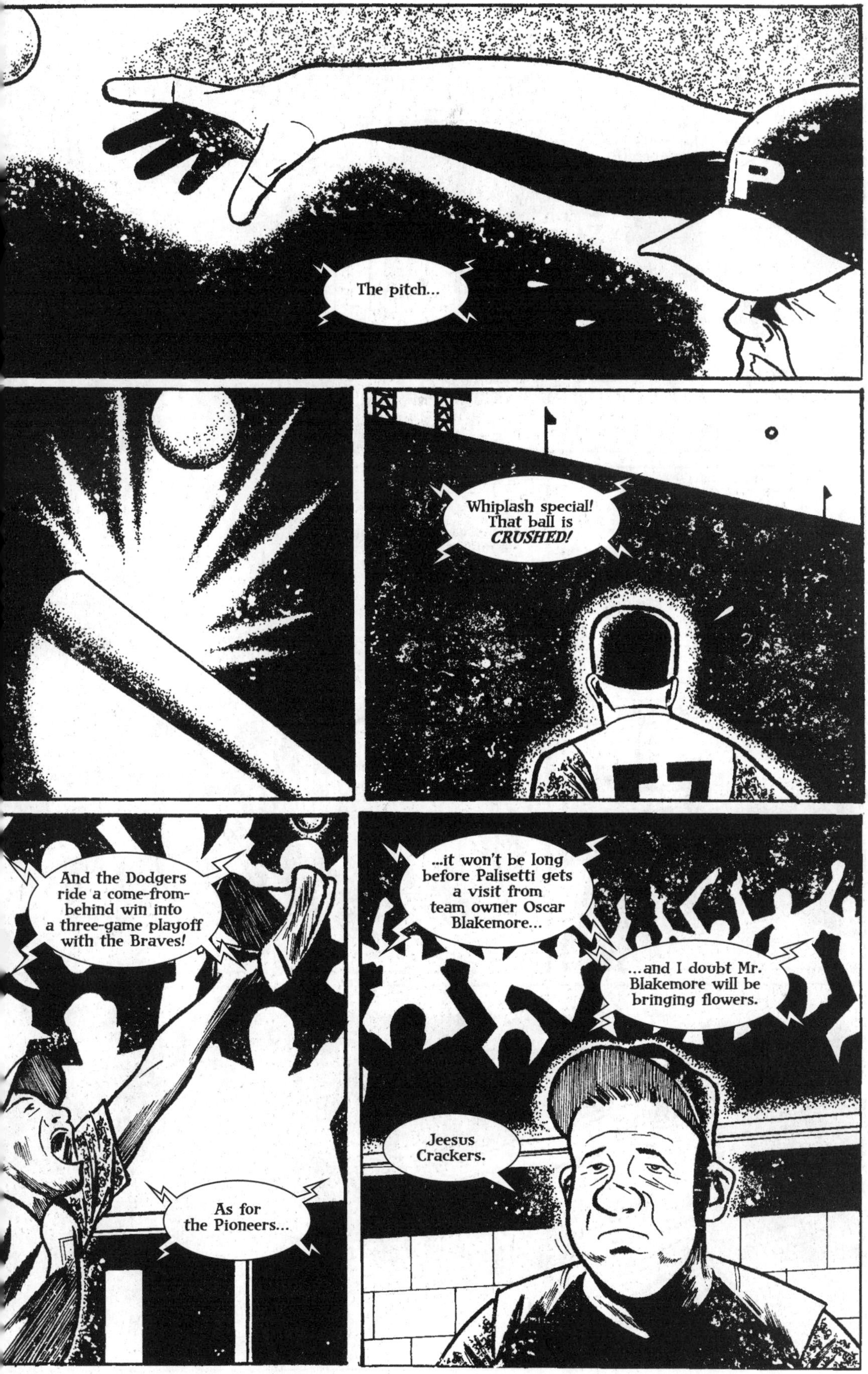
The pitch...
Whiplash special! That ball is *CRUSHED!*
And the Dodgers ride a come-from-behind win into a three-game playoff with the Braves!
As for the Pioneers...
...it won't be long before Palisetti gets a visit from team owner Oscar Blakemore...
...and I doubt Mr. Blakemore will be bringing flowers.
Jeesus Crackers.

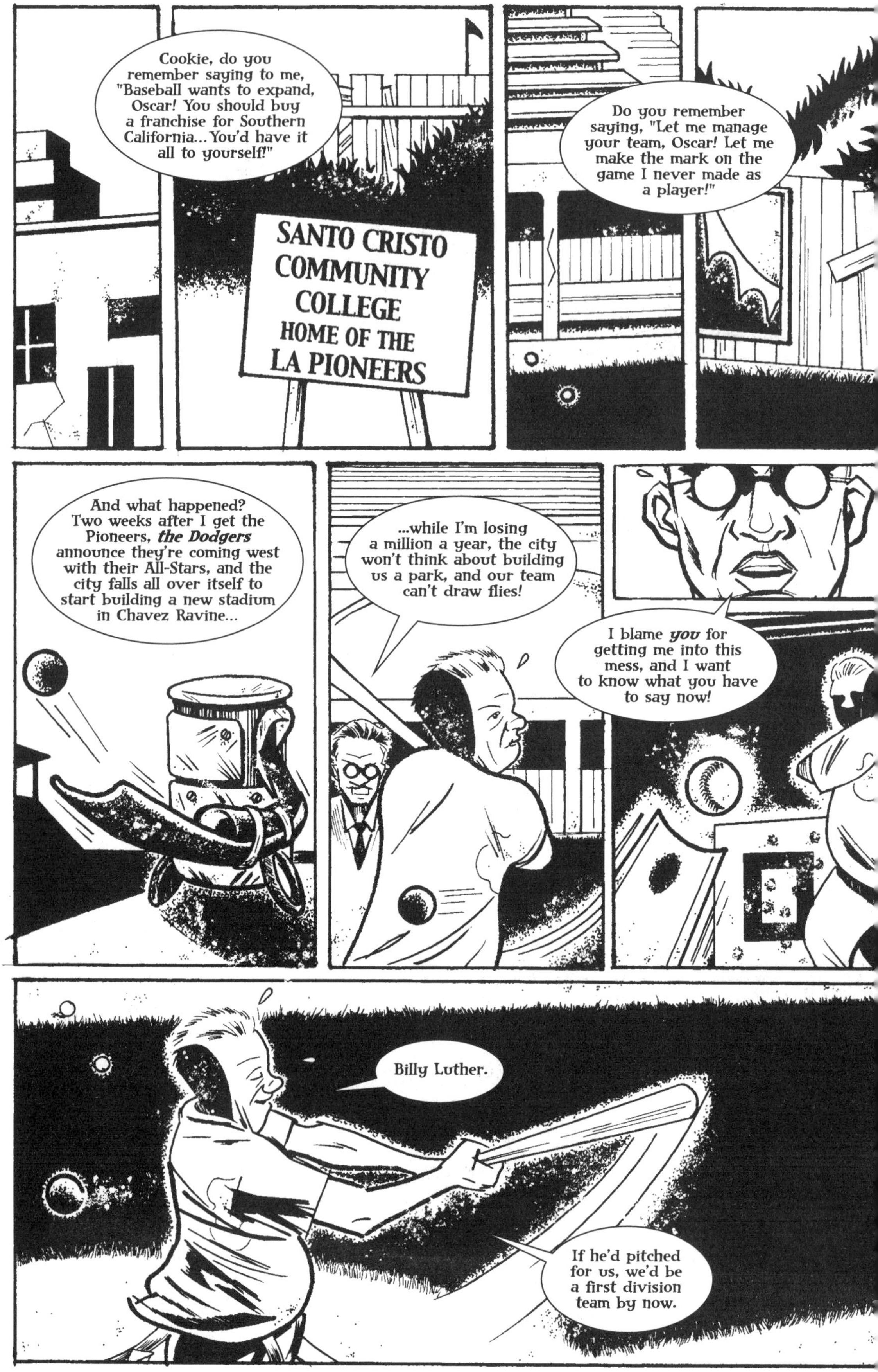
Cookie, do you remember saying to me, "Baseball wants to expand, Oscar! You should buy a franchise for Southern California... You'd have it all to yourself!"
SANTO CRISTO COMMUNITY COLLEGE HOME OF THE LA PIONEERS
Do you remember saying, "Let me manage your team, Oscar! Let me make the mark on the game I never made as a player!"
And what happened? Two weeks after I get the Pioneers, *the Dodgers* announce they're coming west with their All-Stars, and the city falls all over itself to start building a new stadium in Chavez Ravine...
...while I'm losing a million a year, the city won't think about building us a park, and our team can't draw flies!
I blame *you* for getting me into this mess, and I want to know what you have to say now!
Billy Luther.
If he'd pitched for us, we'd be a first division team by now.

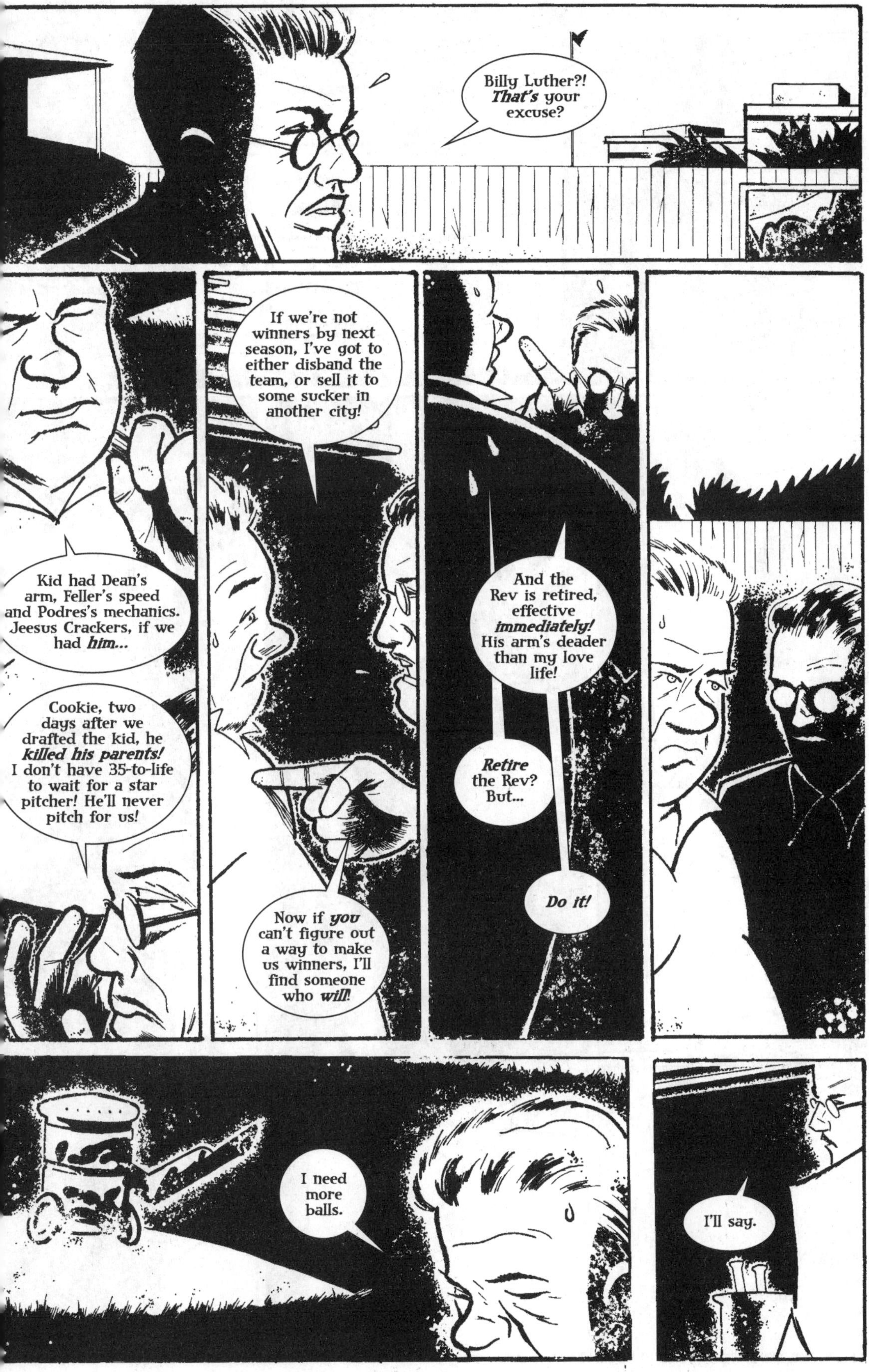

Billy Luther?! *That's* your excuse?
Kid had Dean's arm, Feller's speed and Podres's mechanics. Jeesus Crackers, if we had *him*...
Cookie, two days after we drafted the kid, he *killed his parents!* I don't have 35-to-life to wait for a star pitcher! He'll never pitch for us!
If we're not winners by next season, I've got to either disband the team, or sell it to some sucker in another city!
Now if *you* can't figure out a way to make us winners, I'll find someone who *will!*
And the Rev is retired, effective *immediately!* His arm's deader than my love life!
Retire the Rev? But...
Do it!
I need more balls.
I'll say.

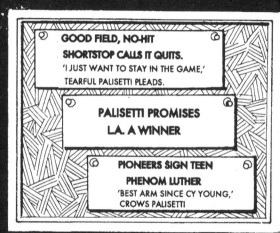

GOOD FIELD, NO-HIT
SHORTSTOP CALLS IT QUITS.
'I JUST WANT TO STAY IN THE GAME,'
TEARFUL PALISETTI PLEADS.

PALISETTI PROMISES
L.A. A WINNER

PIONEERS SIGN TEEN
PHENOM LUTHER
'BEST ARM SINCE CY YOUNG,'
CROWS PALISETTI

Hell of *an arm*, that kid...

...but that's the way the ball bounces.

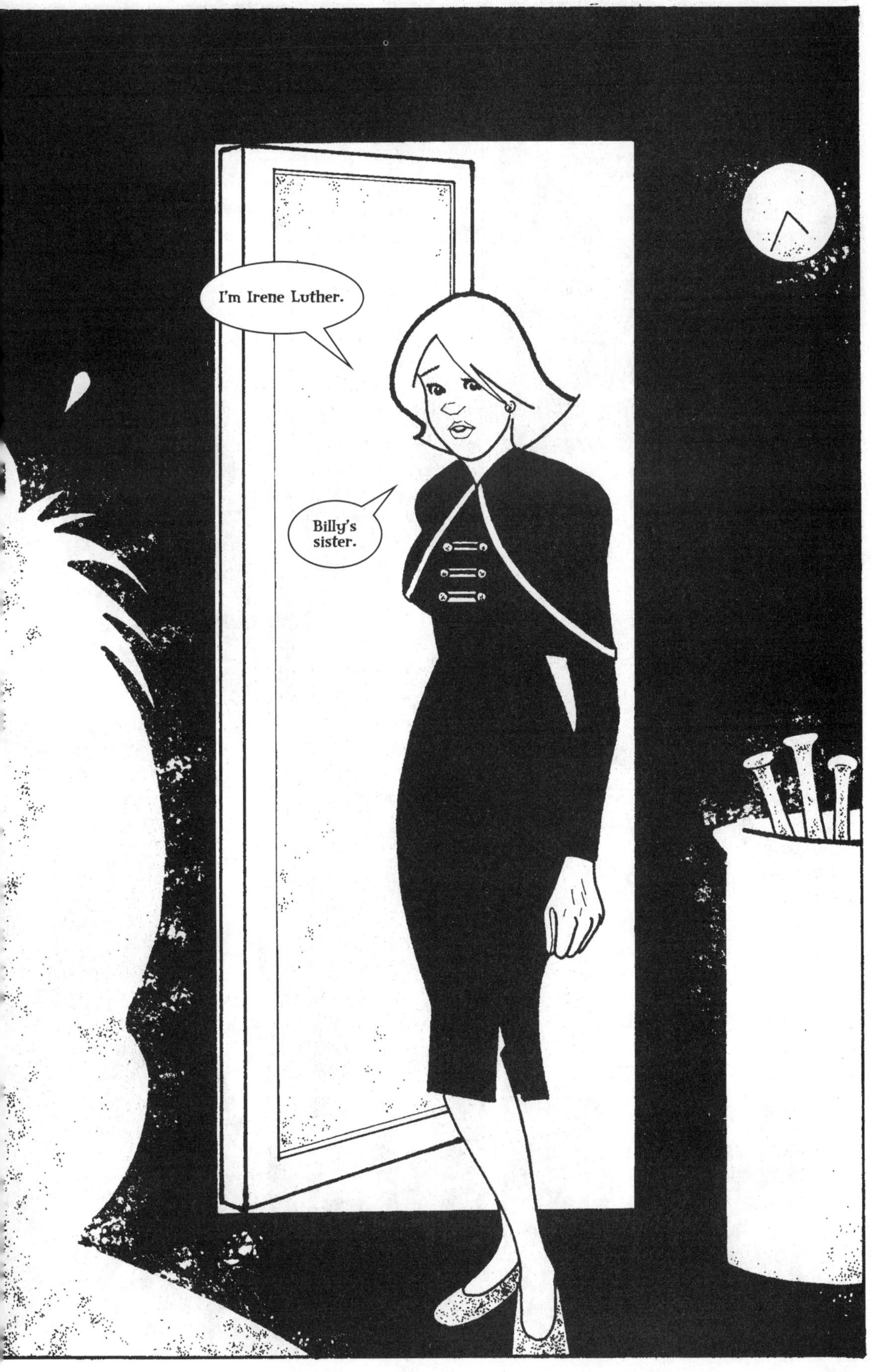
I'm Irene Luther.
Billy's sister.

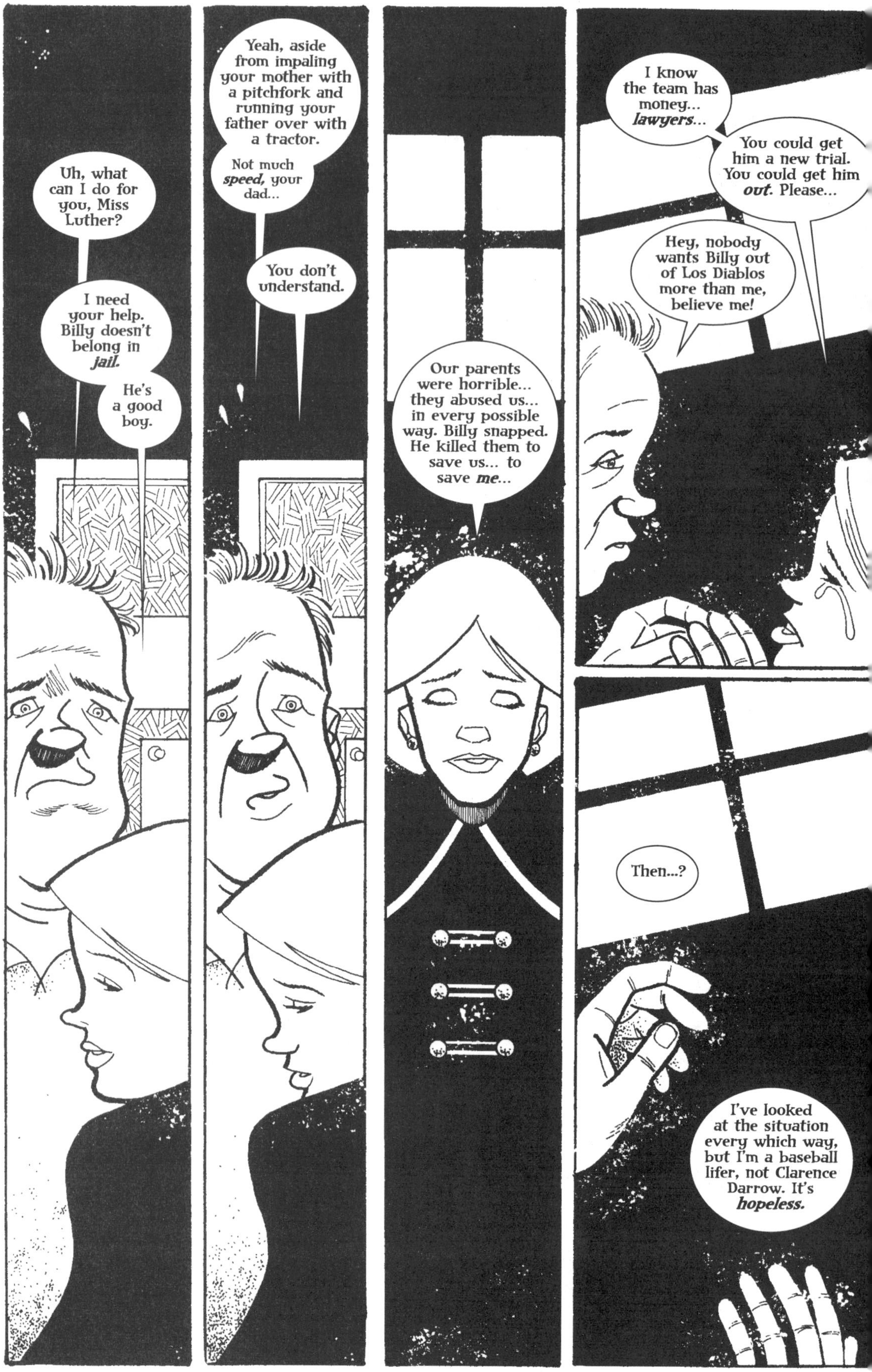

Uh, what can I do for you, Miss Luther?
I need your help. Billy doesn't belong in *jail.*
He's a good boy.
Yeah, aside from impaling your mother with a pitchfork and running your father over with a tractor.
Not much *speed,* your dad...
You don't understand.
Our parents were horrible... they abused us... in every possible way. Billy snapped. He killed them to save us... to save *me*...
I know the team has money... *lawyers*...
You could get him a new trial. You could get him *out*. Please...
Hey, nobody wants Billy out of Los Diablos more than me, believe me!
Then...?
I've looked at the situation every which way, but I'm a baseball lifer, not Clarence Darrow. It's *hopeless.*

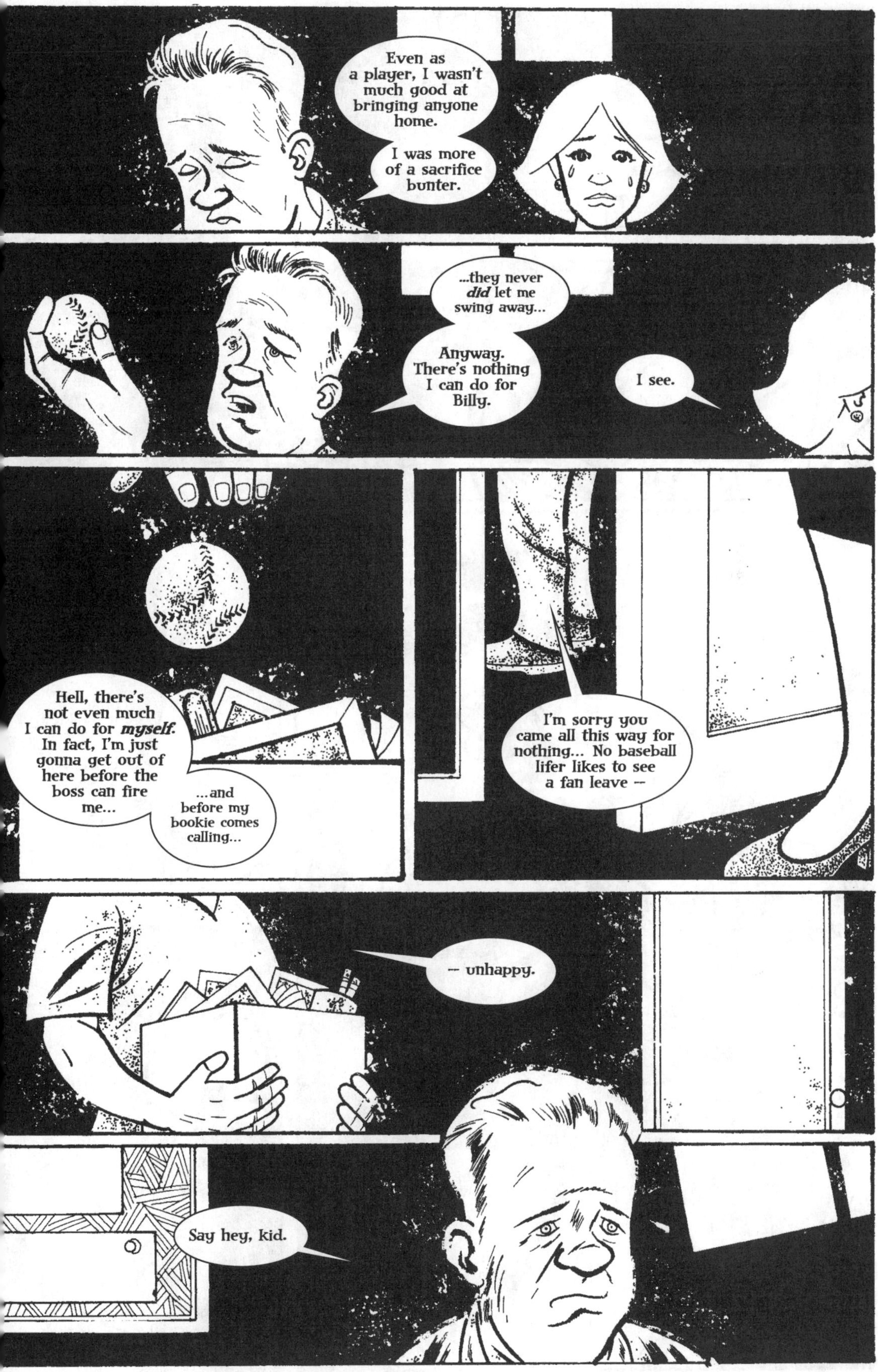

Even as a player, I wasn't much good at bringing anyone home.
I was more of a sacrifice bunter.
...they never *did* let me swing away...
Anyway. There's nothing I can do for Billy.
I see.
Hell, there's not even much I can do for *myself*. In fact, I'm just gonna get out of here before the boss can fire me...
...and before my bookie comes calling...
I'm sorry you came all this way for nothing... No baseball lifer likes to see a fan leave --
-- unhappy.
Say hey, kid.

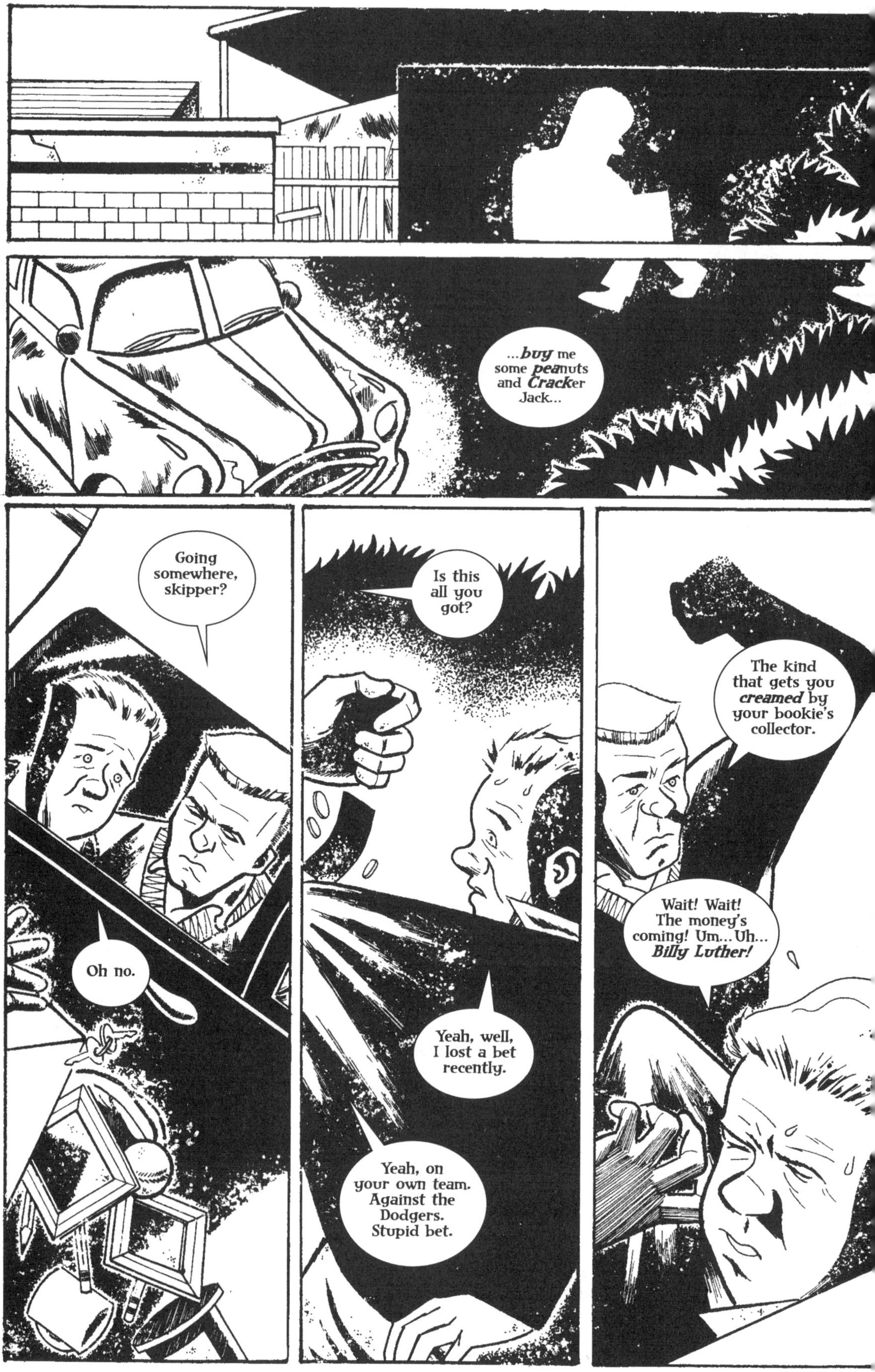
...buy me some peanuts and Cracker Jack...
Going somewhere, skipper?
Oh no.
Is this all you got?
Yeah, well, I lost a bet recently.
Yeah, on your own team. Against the Dodgers. Stupid bet.
The kind that gets you creamed by your bookie's collector.
Wait! Wait! The money's coming! Um...Uh... Billy Luther!

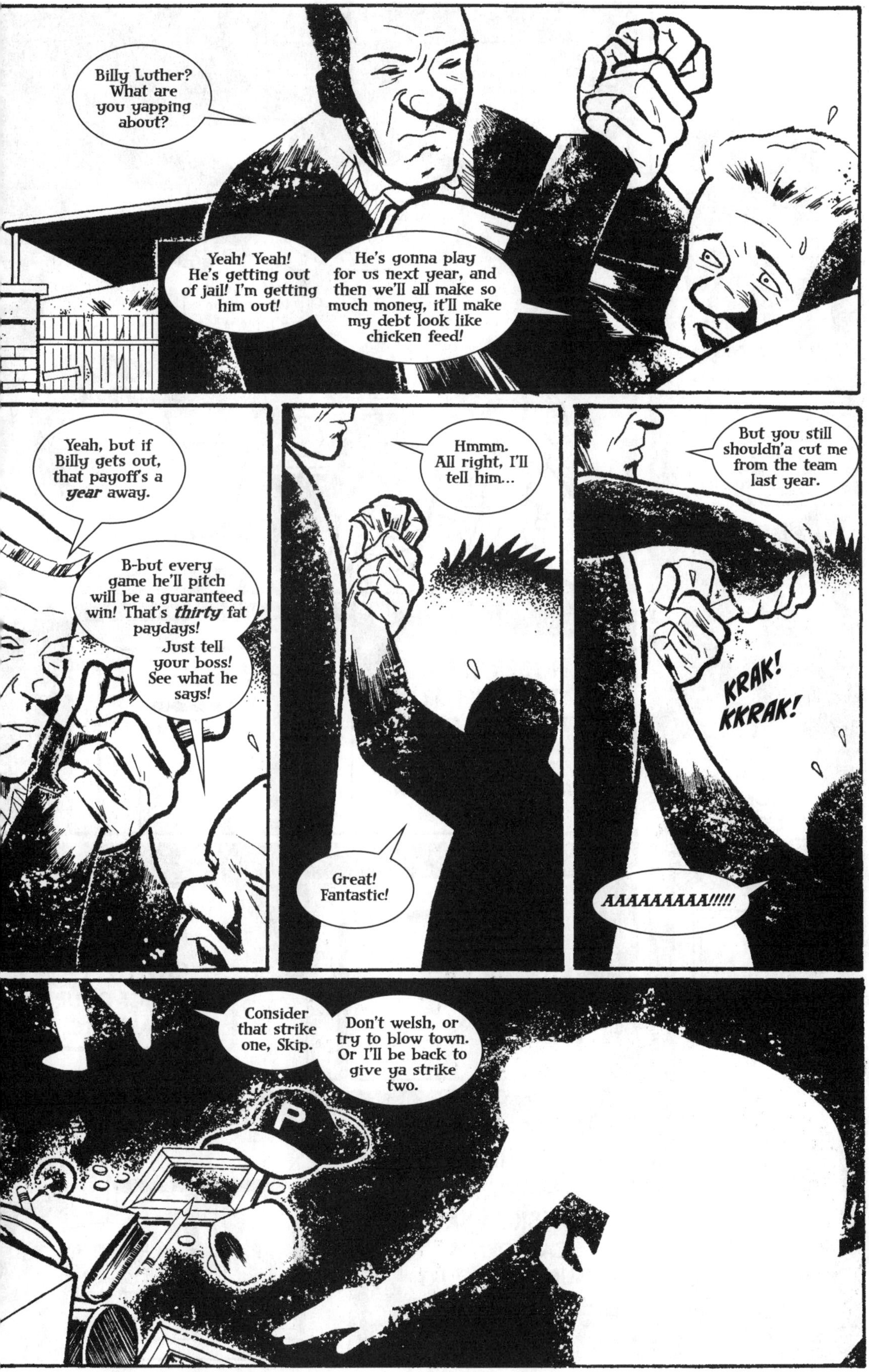
Billy Luther? What are you yapping about?
Yeah! Yeah! He's getting out of jail! I'm getting him out!
He's gonna play for us next year, and then we'll all make so much money, it'll make my debt look like chicken feed!
Yeah, but if Billy gets out, that payoff's a *year* away.
B-but every game he'll pitch will be a guaranteed win! That's *thirty* fat paydays!
Just tell your boss! See what he says!
Hmmm. All right, I'll tell him...
Great! Fantastic!
But you still shouldn'a cut me from the team last year.
KRAK! KKRAK!
AAAAAAAAA!!!!!
Consider that strike one, Skip.
Don't welsh, or try to blow town. Or I'll be back to give ya strike two.
P

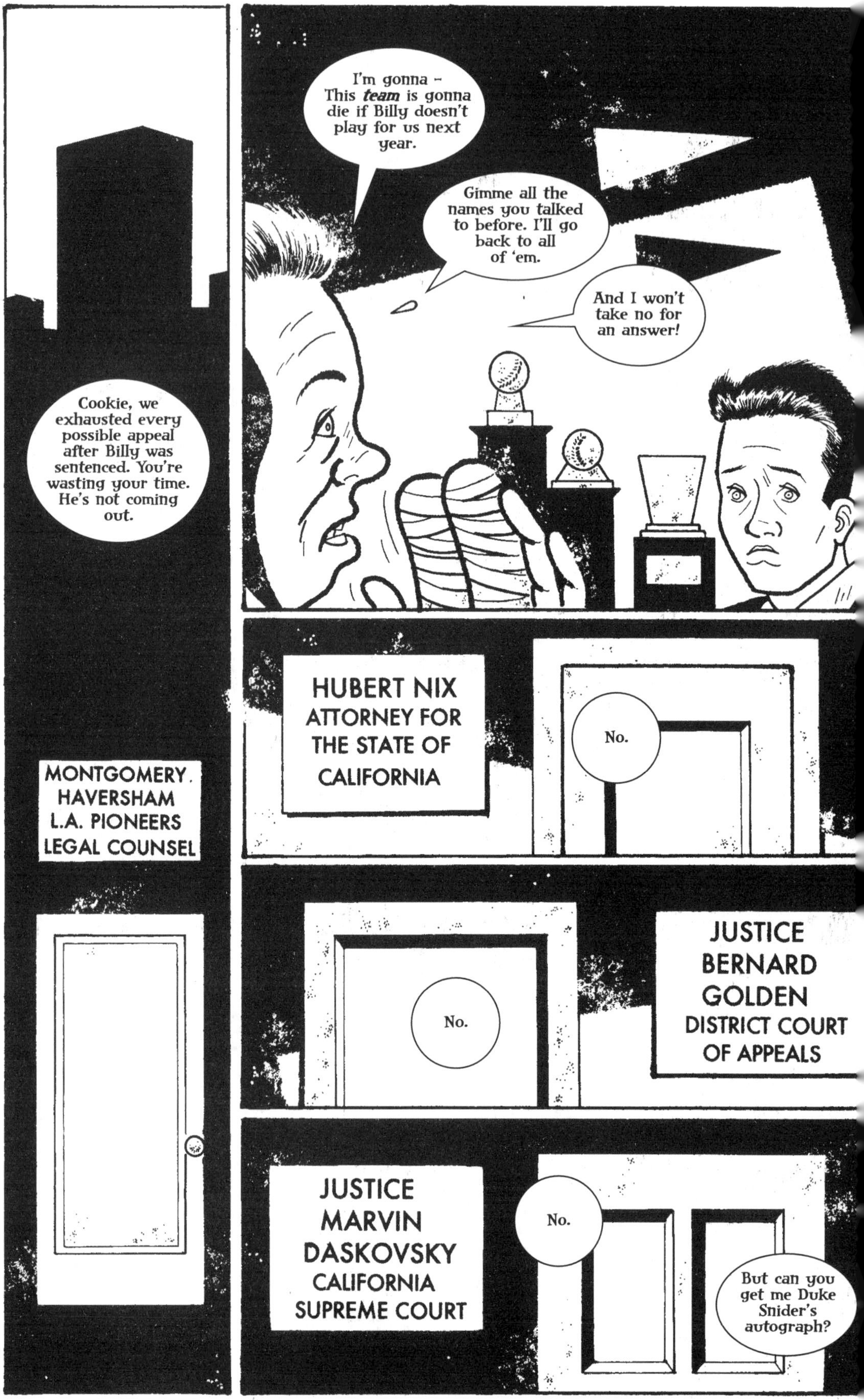

Cookie, we exhausted every possible appeal after Billy was sentenced. You're wasting your time. He's not coming out.
MONTGOMERY HAVERSHAM L.A. PIONEERS LEGAL COUNSEL
I'm gonna – This *team* is gonna die if Billy doesn't play for us next year.
Gimme all the names you talked to before. I'll go back to all of 'em.
And I won't take no for an answer!
HUBERT NIX ATTORNEY FOR THE STATE OF CALIFORNIA
No.
No.
JUSTICE BERNARD GOLDEN DISTRICT COURT OF APPEALS
JUSTICE MARVIN DASKOVSKY CALIFORNIA SUPREME COURT
No.
But can you get me Duke Snider's autograph?

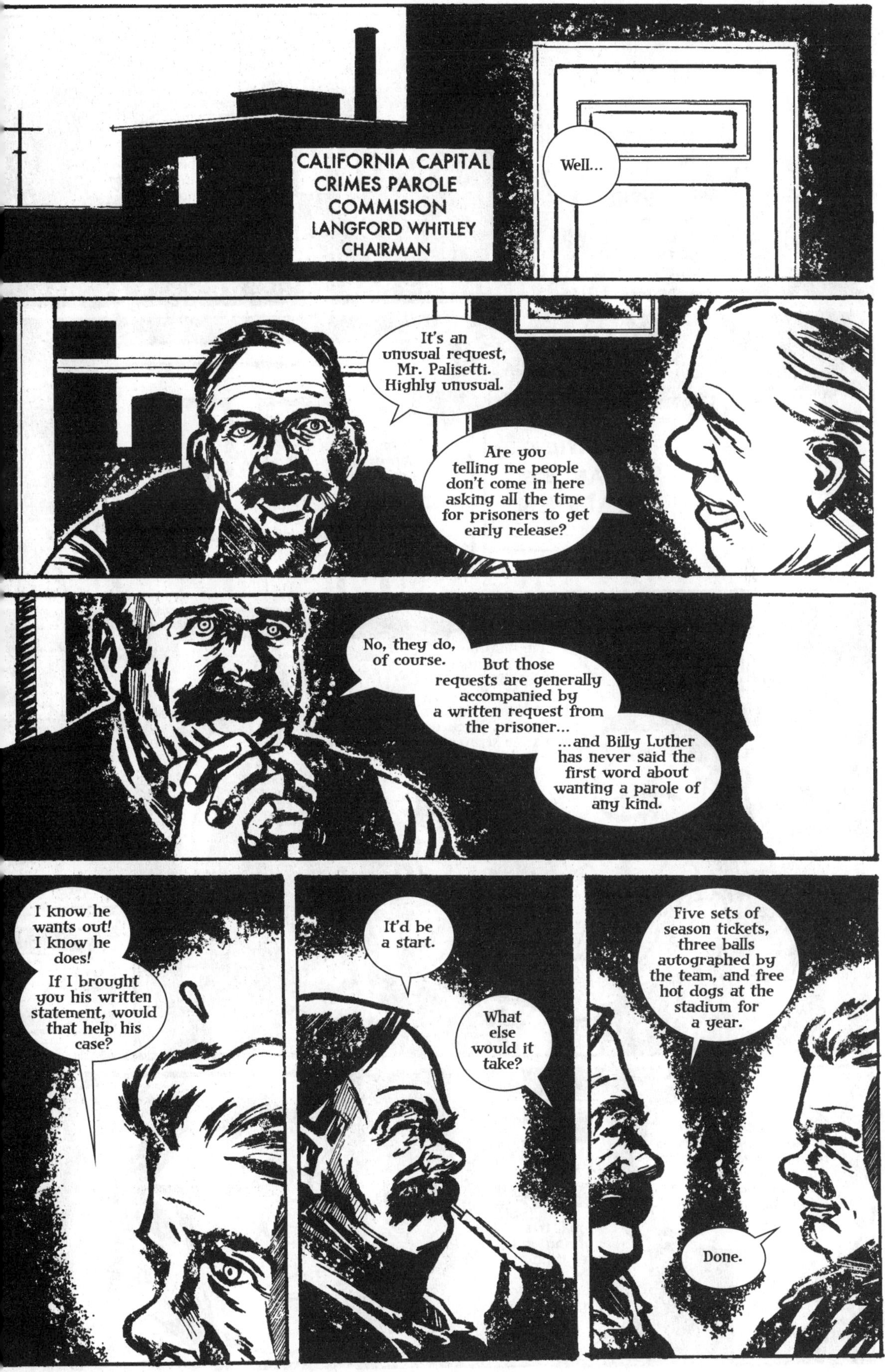
CALIFORNIA CAPITAL CRIMES PAROLE COMMISION LANGFORD WHITLEY CHAIRMAN
Well...
It's an unusual request, Mr. Palisetti. Highly unusual.
Are you telling me people don't come in here asking all the time for prisoners to get early release?
No, they do, of course.
But those requests are generally accompanied by a written request from the prisoner...
...and Billy Luther has never said the first word about wanting a parole of any kind.
I know he wants out! I know he does!
If I brought you his written statement, would that help his case?
It'd be a start.
What else would it take?
Five sets of season tickets, three balls autographed by the team, and free hot dogs at the stadium for a year.
Done.

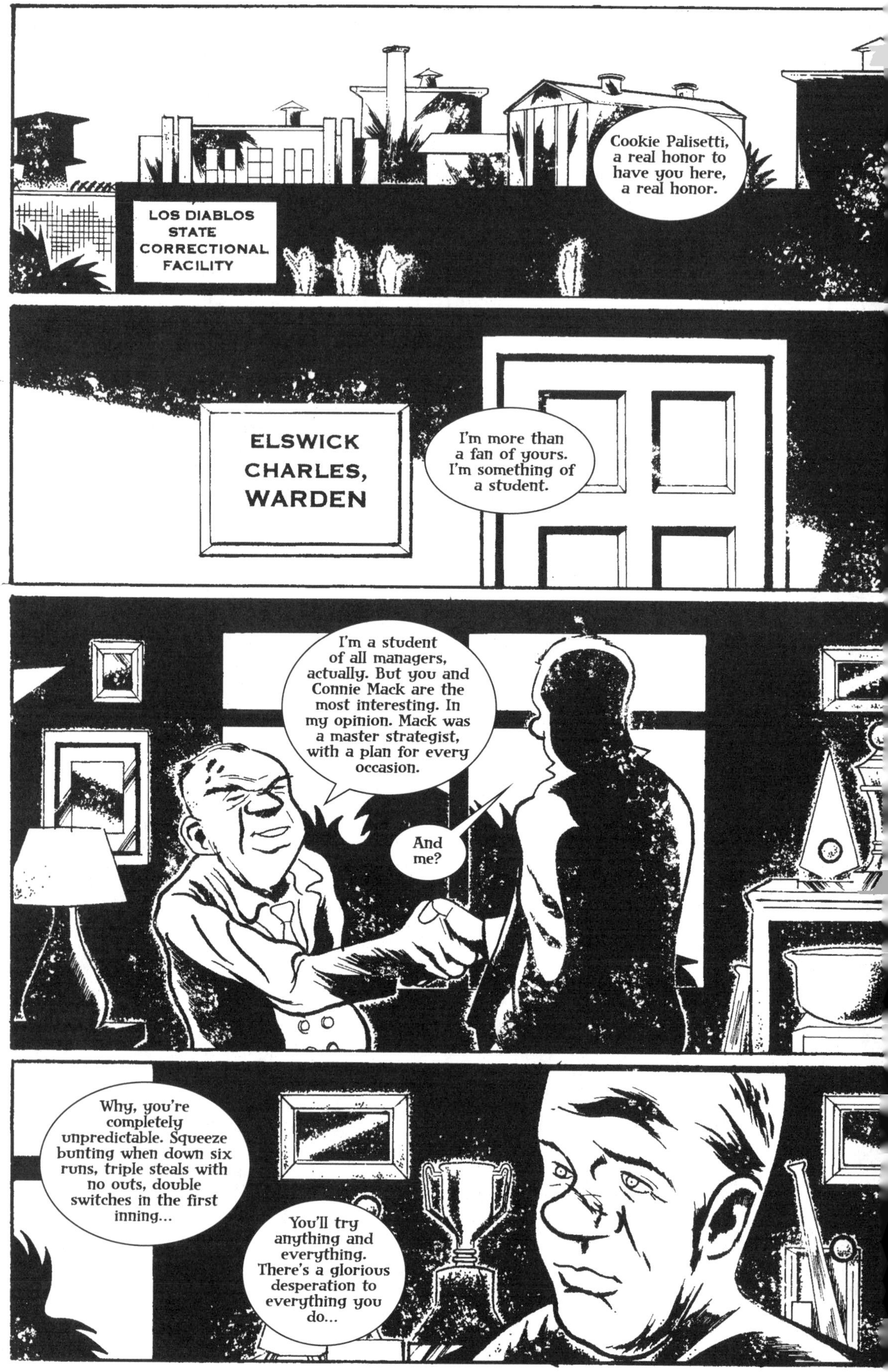
LOS DIABLOS STATE CORRECTIONAL FACILITY
Cookie Palisetti, a real honor to have you here, a real honor.
ELSWICK CHARLES, WARDEN
I'm more than a fan of yours. I'm something of a student.
I'm a student of all managers, actually. But you and Connie Mack are the most interesting. In my opinion. Mack was a master strategist, with a plan for every occasion.
And me?
Why, you're completely unpredictable. Squeeze bunting when down six runs, triple steals with no outs, double switches in the first inning...
You'll try anything and everything. There's a glorious desperation to everything you do...

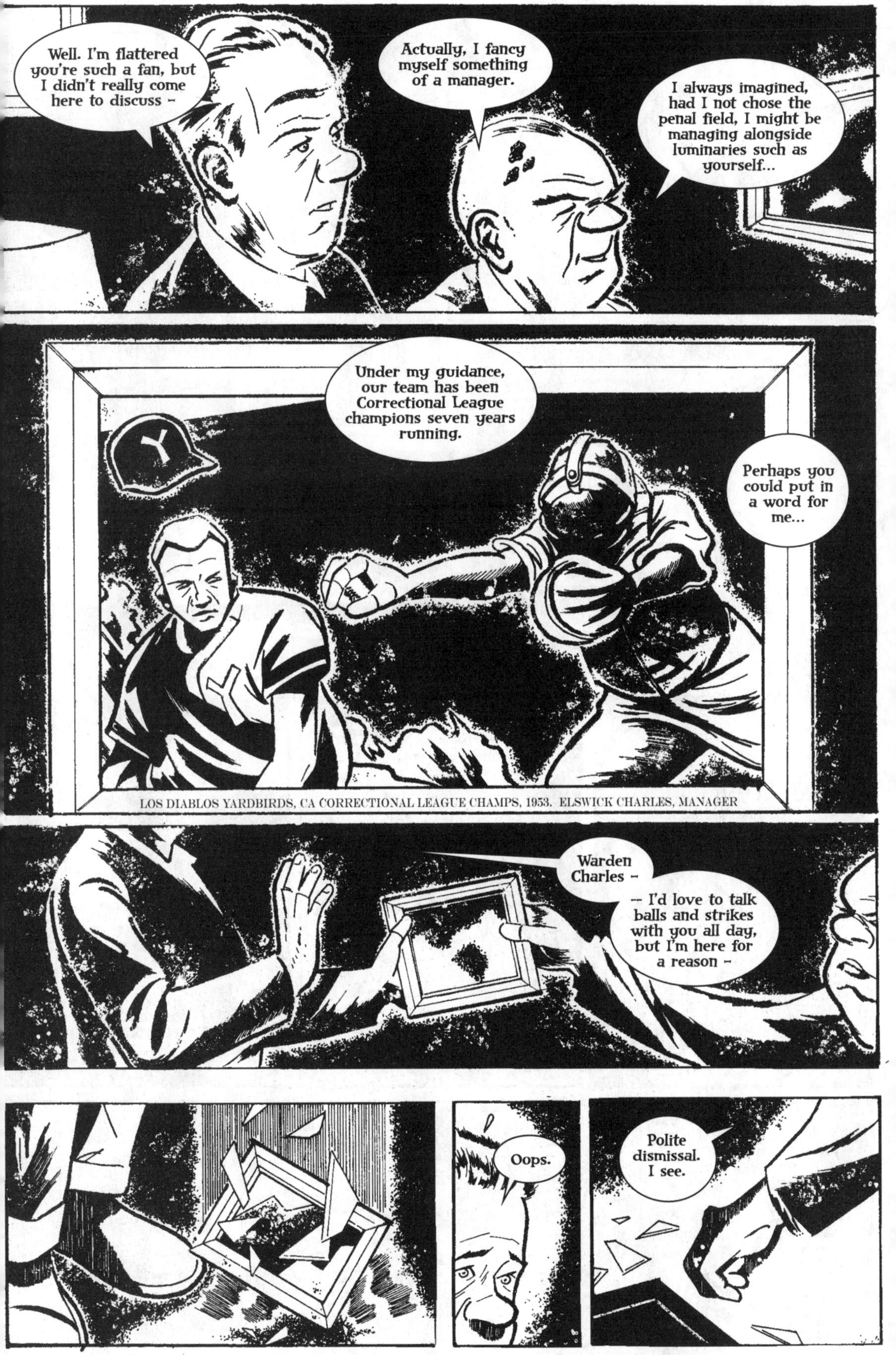
Well. I'm flattered you're such a fan, but I didn't really come here to discuss –
Actually, I fancy myself something of a manager.
I always imagined, had I not chose the penal field, I might be managing alongside luminaries such as yourself...
Under my guidance, our team has been Correctional League champions seven years running.
Perhaps you could put in a word for me...
LOS DIABLOS YARDBIRDS, CA CORRECTIONAL LEAGUE CHAMPS, 1953. ELSWICK CHARLES, MANAGER
Warden Charles –
– I'd love to talk balls and strikes with you all day, but I'm here for a reason –
Oops.
Polite dismissal. I see.

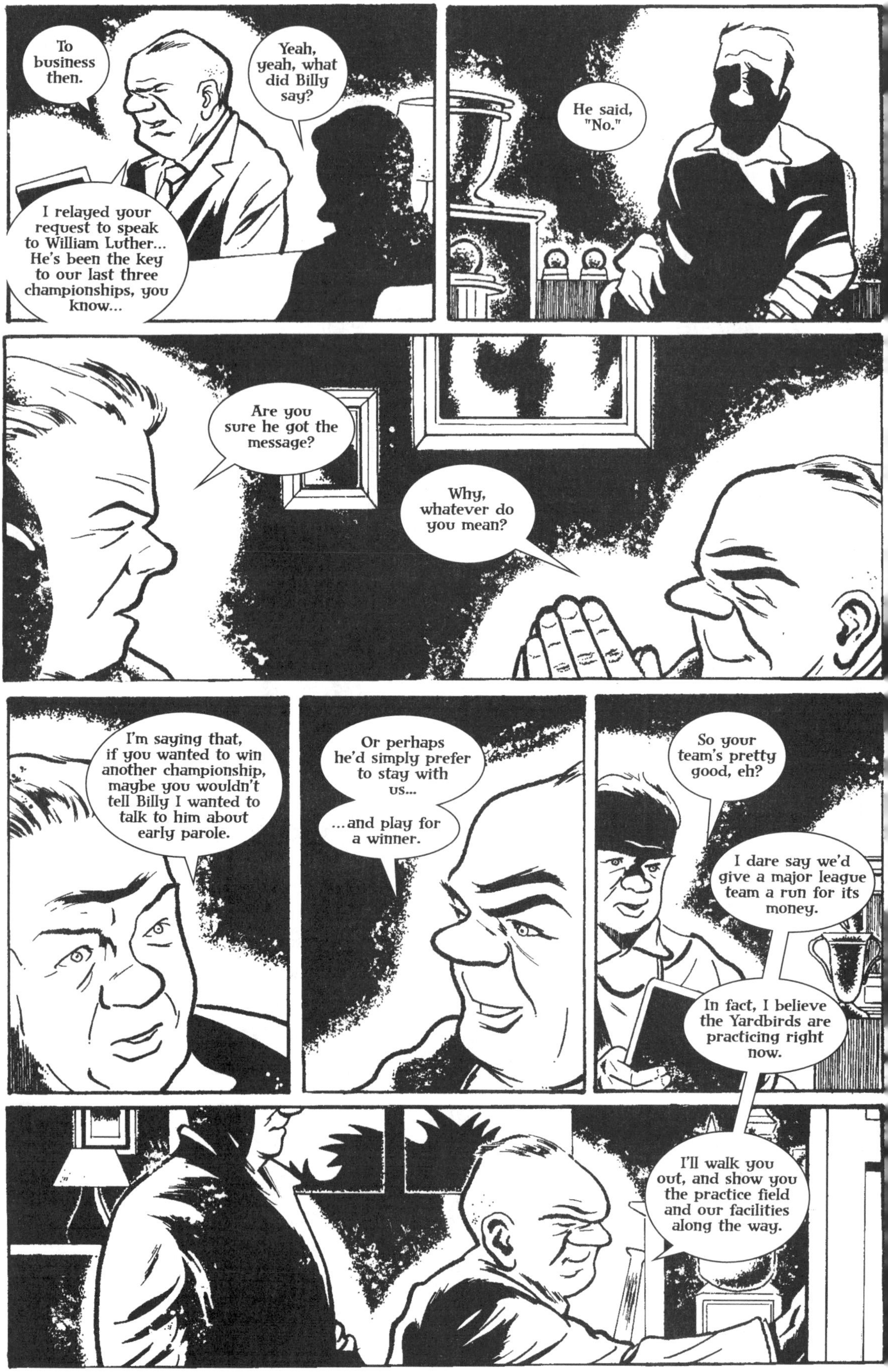

To business then.
Yeah, yeah, what did Billy say?
I relayed your request to speak to William Luther... He's been the key to our last three championships, you know...
He said, "No."
Are you sure he got the message?
Why, whatever do you mean?
I'm saying that, if you wanted to win another championship, maybe you wouldn't tell Billy I wanted to talk to him about early parole.
Or perhaps he'd simply prefer to stay with us...
...and play for a winner.
So your team's pretty good, eh?
I dare say we'd give a major league team a run for its money.
In fact, I believe the Yardbirds are practicing right now.
I'll walk you out, and show you the practice field and our facilities along the way.

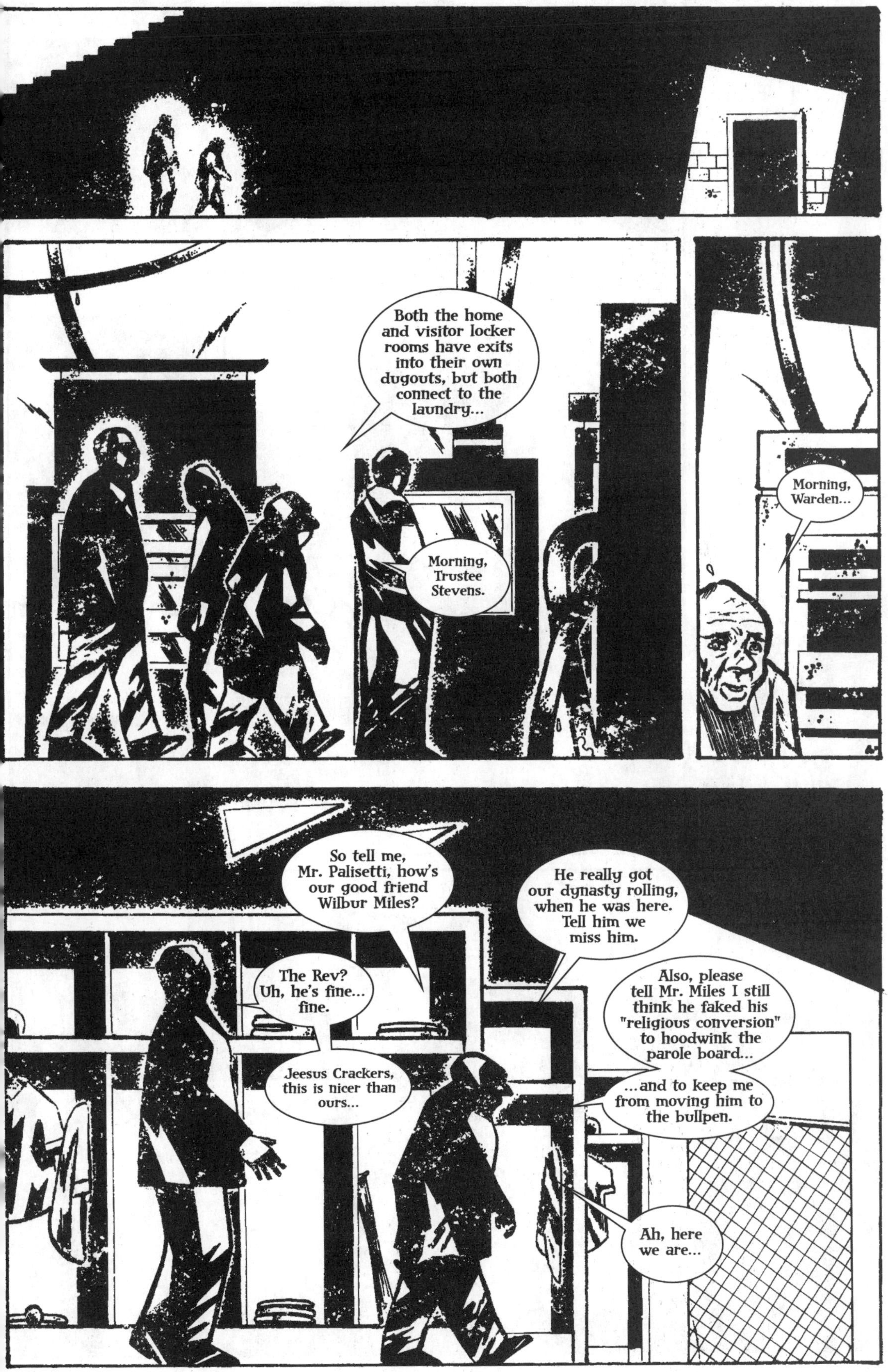
Both the home and visitor locker rooms have exits into their own dugouts, but both connect to the laundry...
Morning, Trustee Stevens.
Morning, Warden...
So tell me, Mr. Palisetti, how's our good friend Wilbur Miles?
The Rev? Uh, he's fine... fine.
He really got our dynasty rolling, when he was here. Tell him we miss him.
Jeesus Crackers, this is nicer than ours...
Also, please tell Mr. Miles I still think he faked his "religious conversion" to hoodwink the parole board...
...and to keep me from moving him to the bullpen.
Ah, here we are...

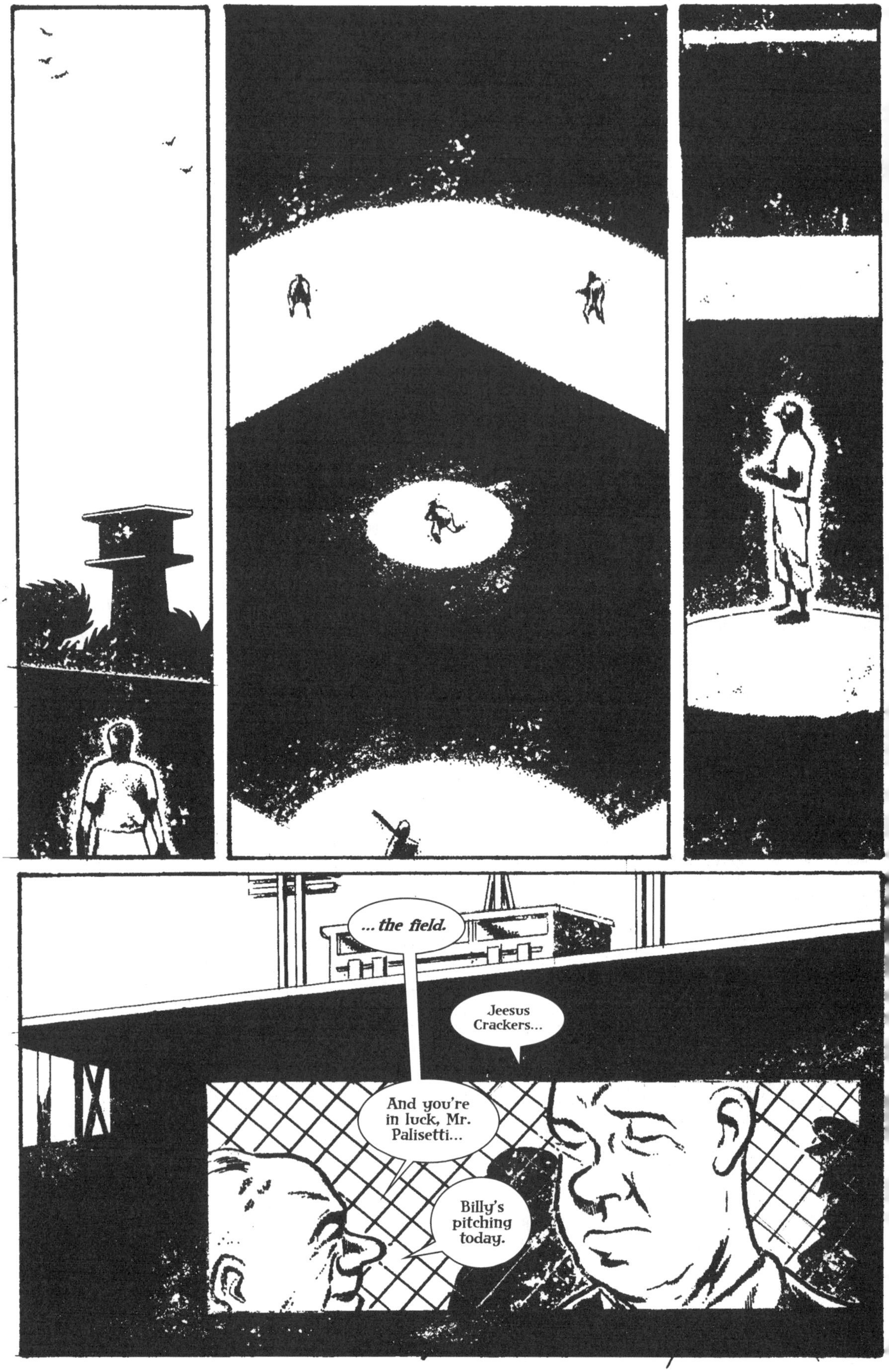

...the field.
Jeesus Crackers...
And you're in luck, Mr. Palisetti...
Billy's pitching today.

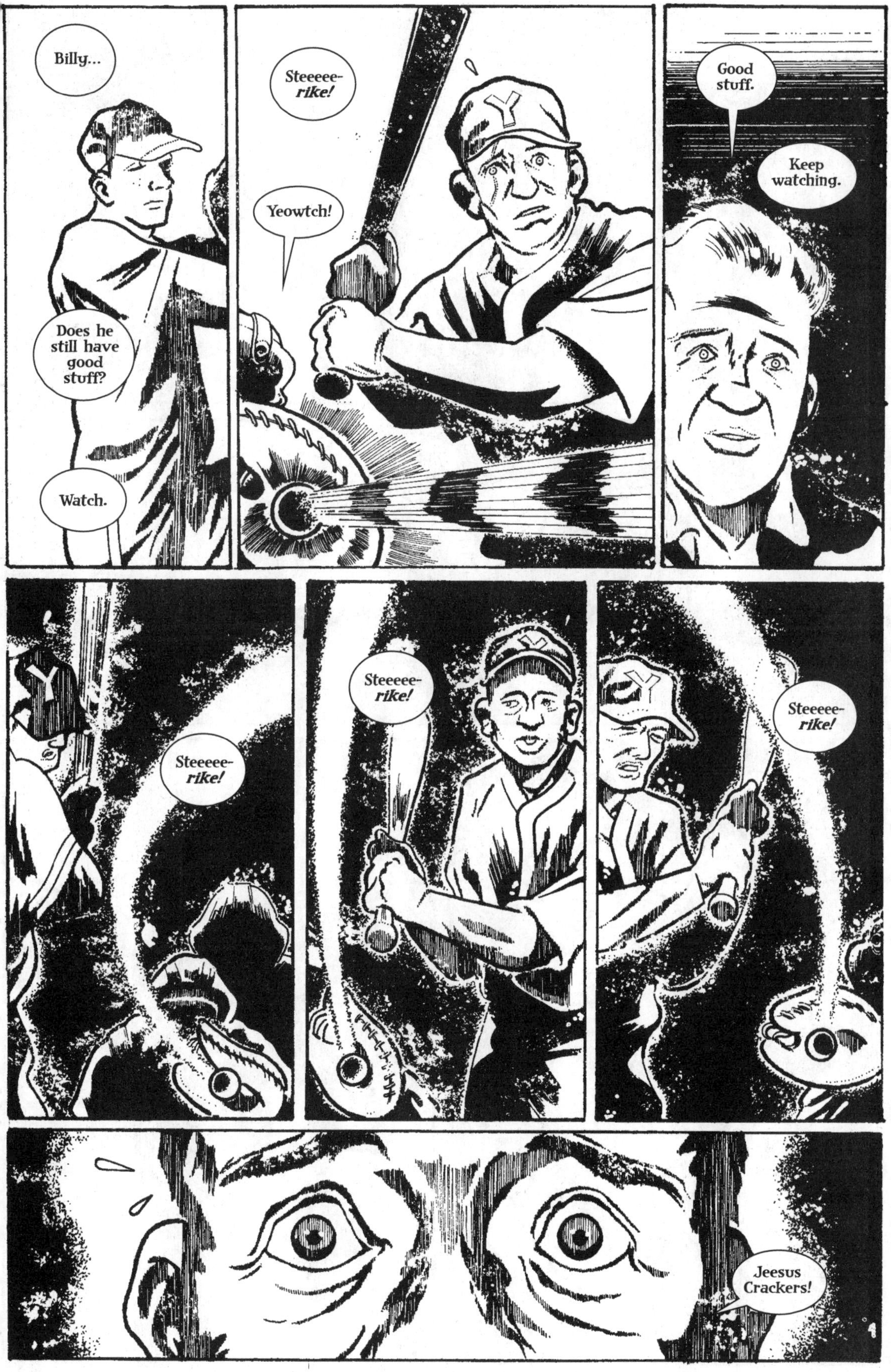
Billy...
Does he still have good stuff?
Watch.
Steeeee-*rike!*
Yeowtch!
Good stuff.
Keep watching.
Steeeee-*rike!*
Steeeee-*rike!*
Steeeee-*rike!*
Jeesus Crackers!

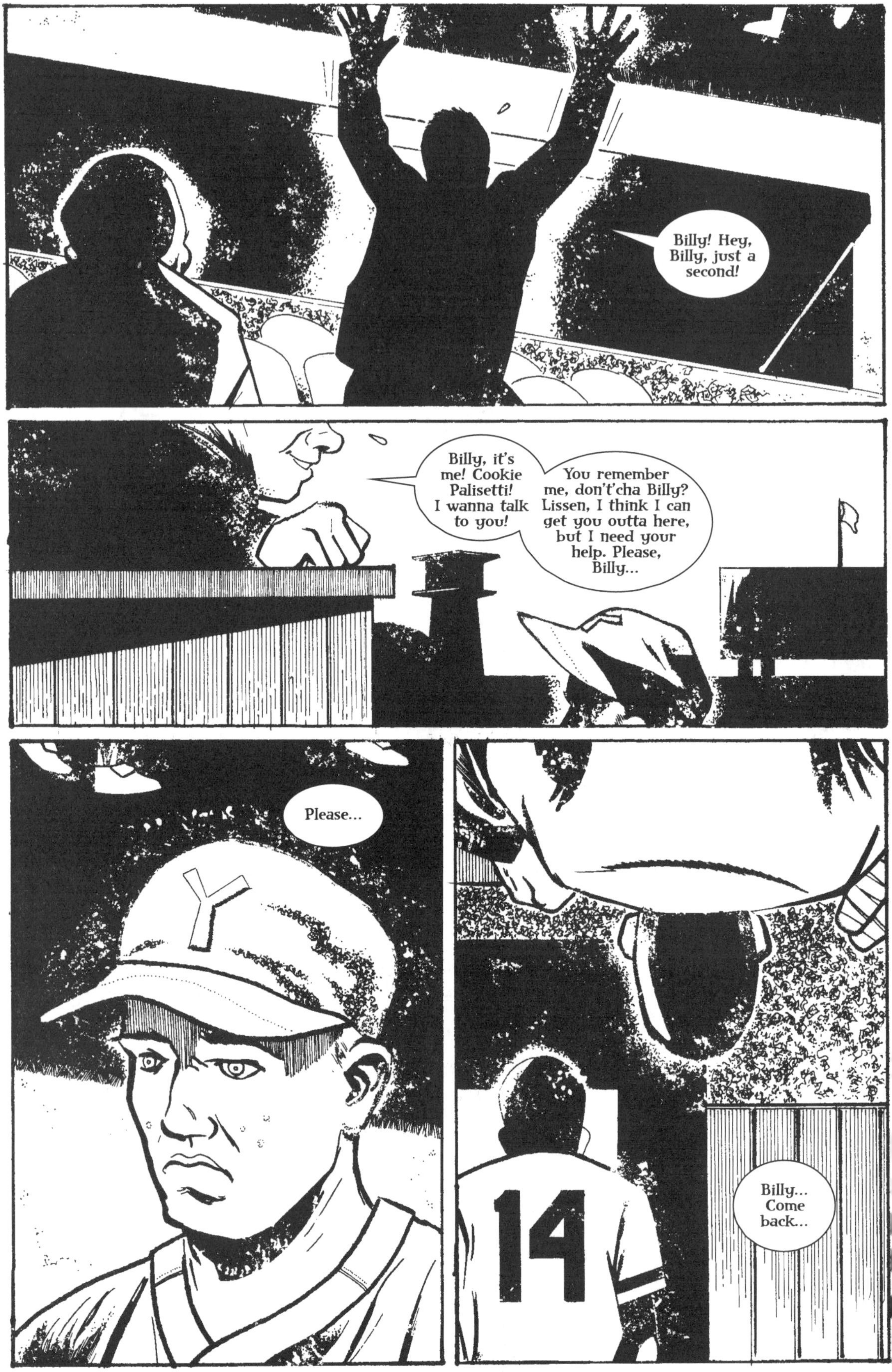

Billy! Hey, Billy, just a second!
Billy, it's me! Cookie Palisetti! I wanna talk to you!
You remember me, don't'cha Billy? Lissen, I think I can get you outta here, but I need your help. Please, Billy...
Please...
14
Billy... Come back...

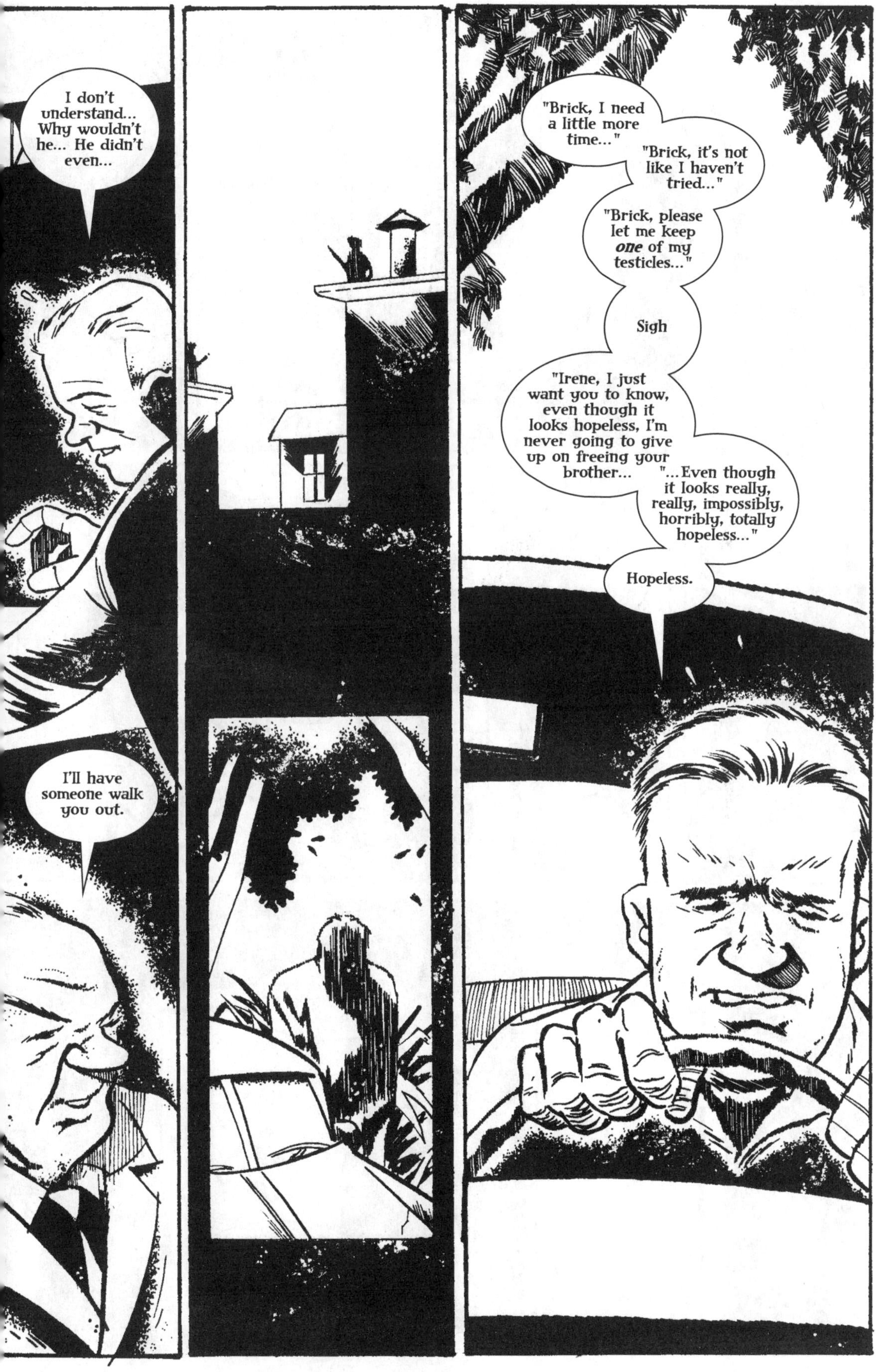
I don't understand... Why wouldn't he... He didn't even...
I'll have someone walk you out.
"Brick, I need a little more time..."
"Brick, it's not like I haven't tried..."
"Brick, please let me keep *one* of my testicles..."
Sigh
"Irene, I just want you to know, even though it looks hopeless, I'm never going to give up on freeing your brother...
"...Even though it looks really, really, impossibly, horribly, totally hopeless..."
Hopeless.

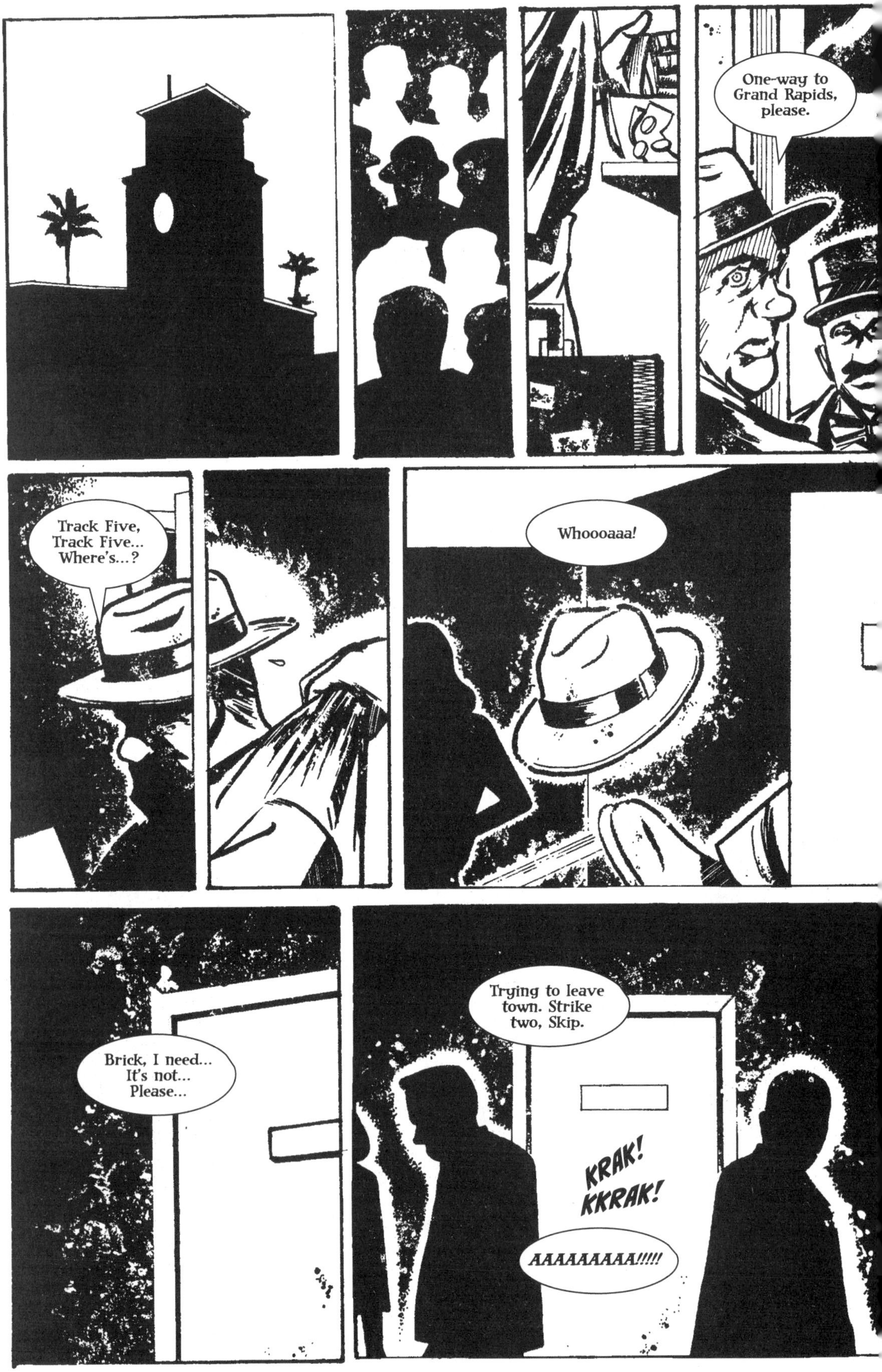
One-way to Grand Rapids, please.
Track Five, Track Five... Where's...?
Whoooaaa!
Brick, I need... It's not... Please...
Trying to leave town. Strike two, Skip.
KRAK! KKRAK!
AAAAAAAAA!!!!!

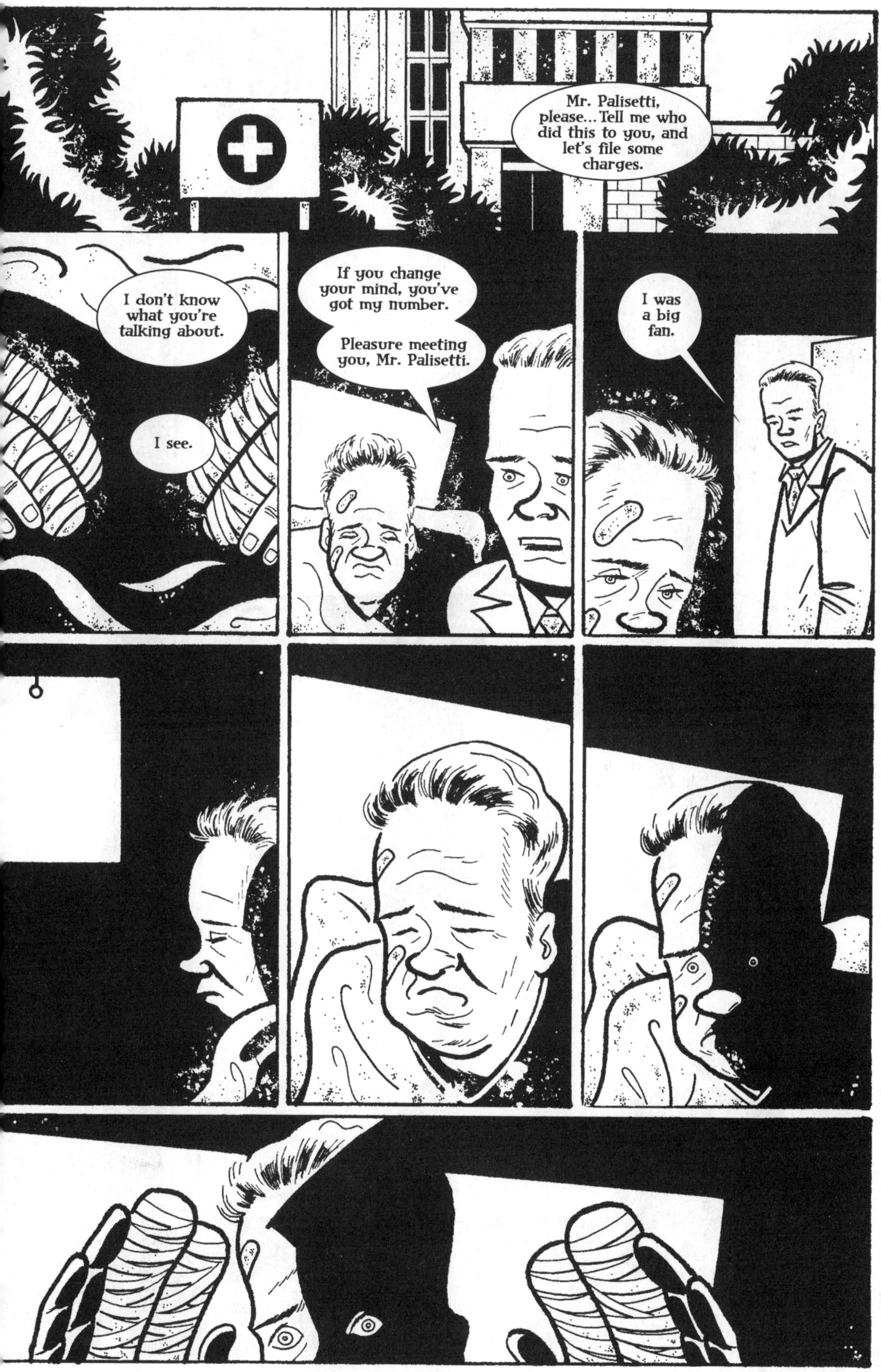
Mr. Palisetti, please... Tell me who did this to you, and let's file some charges.
I don't know what you're talking about.
I see.
If you change your mind, you've got my number.
Pleasure meeting you, Mr. Palisetti.
I was a big fan.

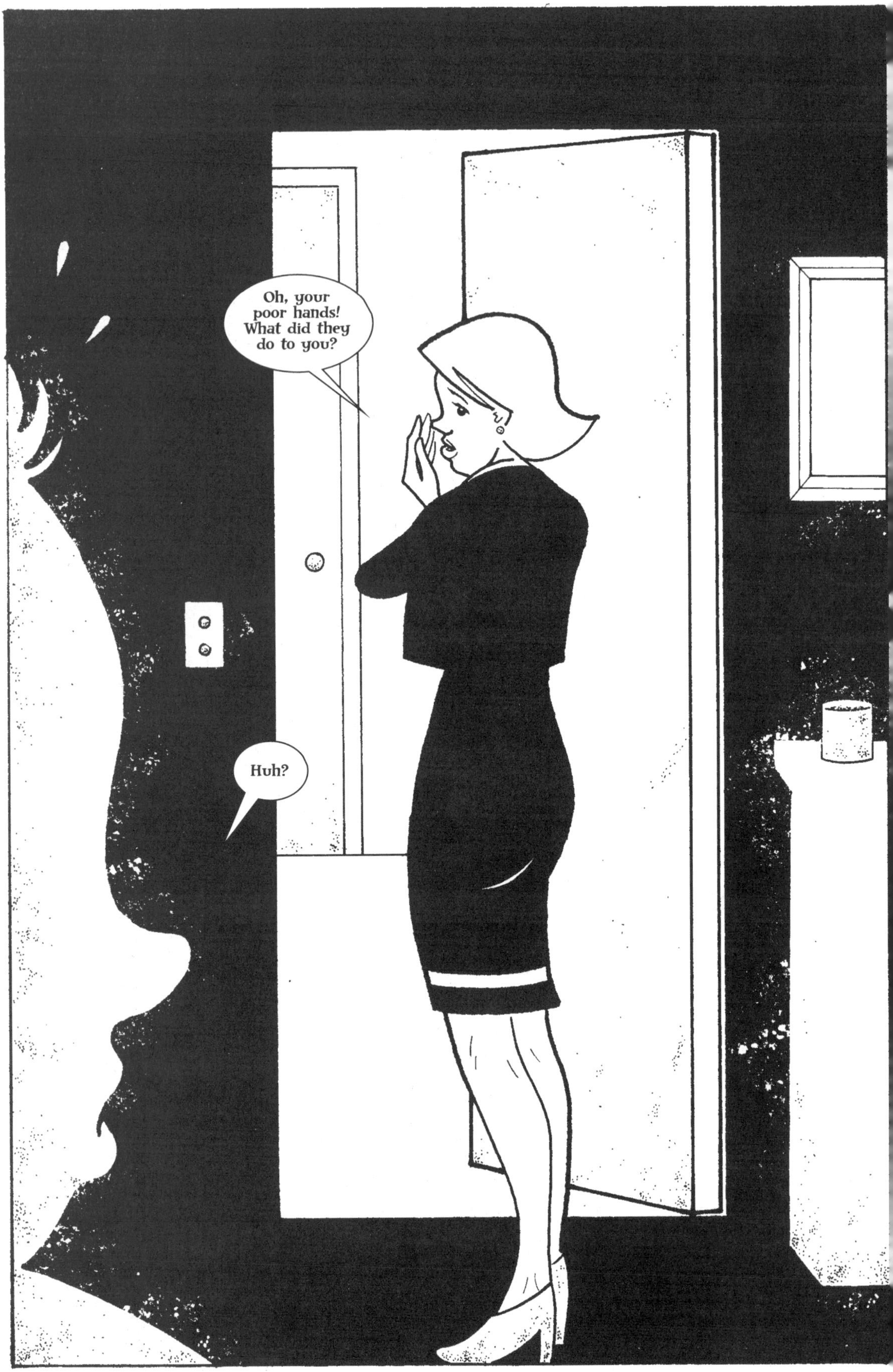
Oh, your poor hands! What did they do to you?
Huh?

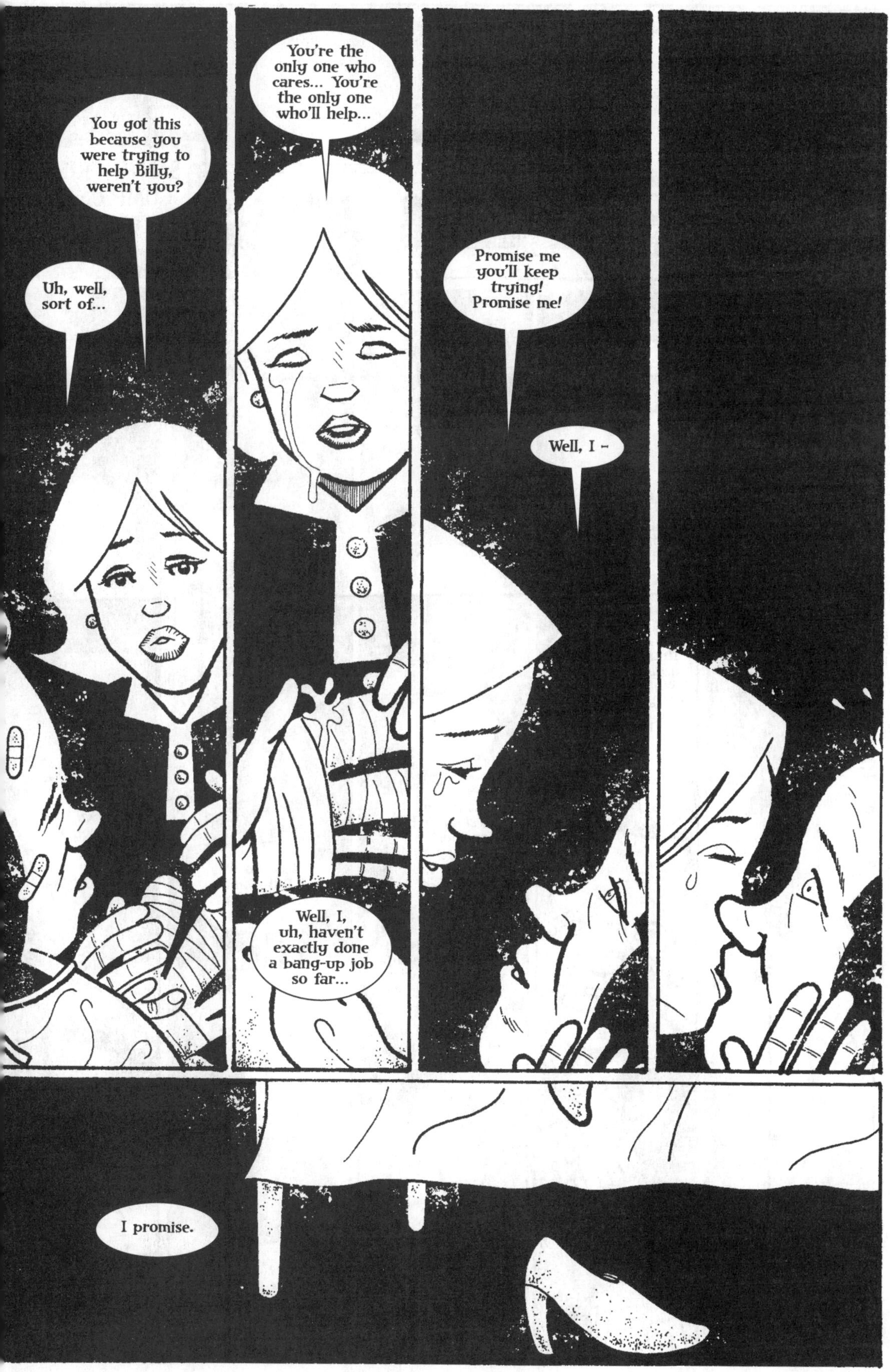
You got this because you were trying to help Billy, weren't you?
Uh, well, sort of...
You're the only one who cares... You're the only one who'll help...
Well, I, uh, haven't exactly done a bang-up job so far...
Promise me you'll keep trying! Promise me!
Well, I –
I promise.

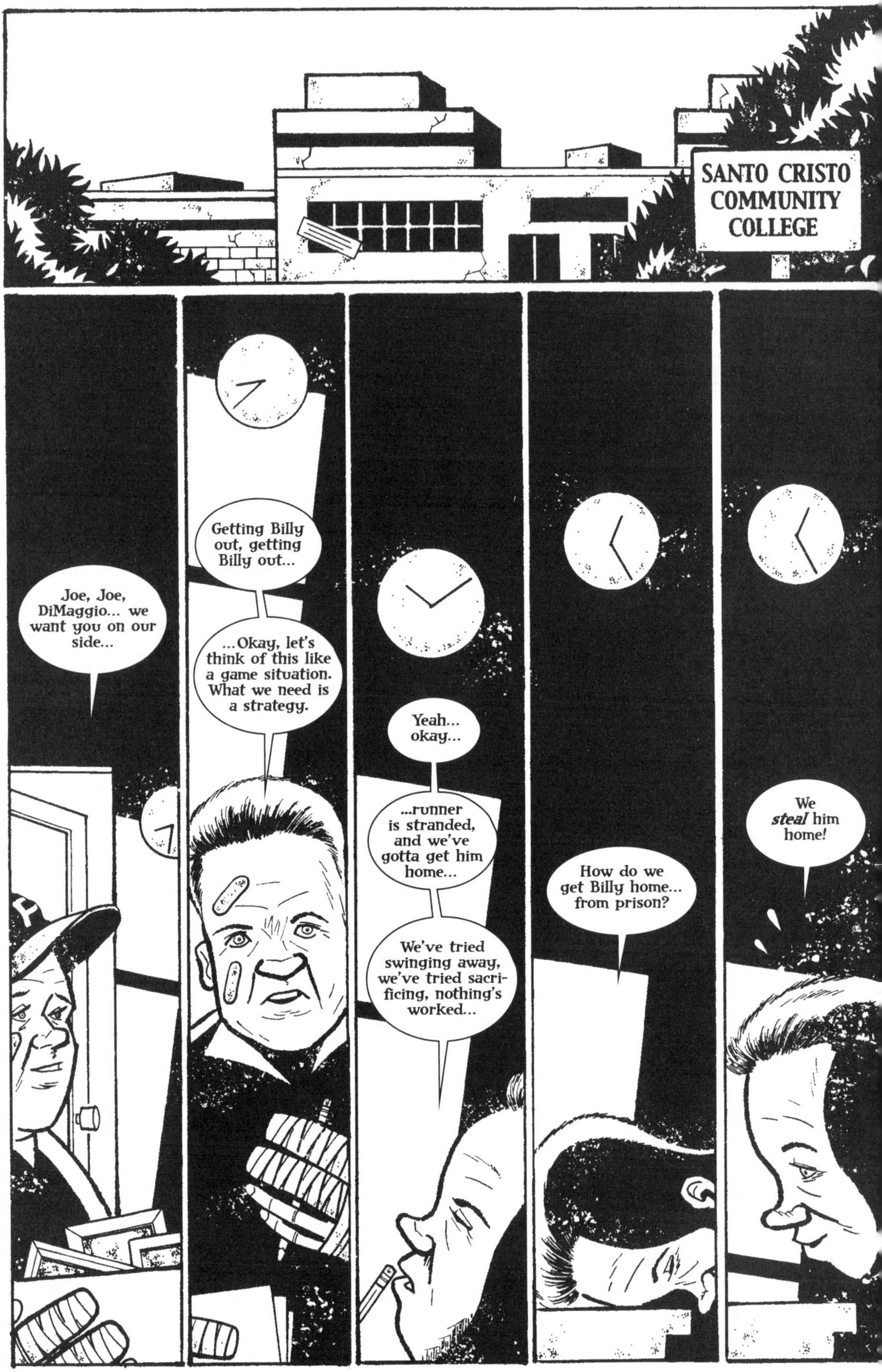
SANTO CRISTO COMMUNITY COLLEGE
Joe, Joe, DiMaggio... we want you on our side...
Getting Billy out, getting Billy out...
...Okay, let's think of this like a game situation. What we need is a strategy.
Yeah... okay...
...runner is stranded, and we've gotta get him home...
We've tried swinging away, we've tried sacri-ficing, nothing's worked...
How do we get Billy home... from prison?
We *steal* him home!

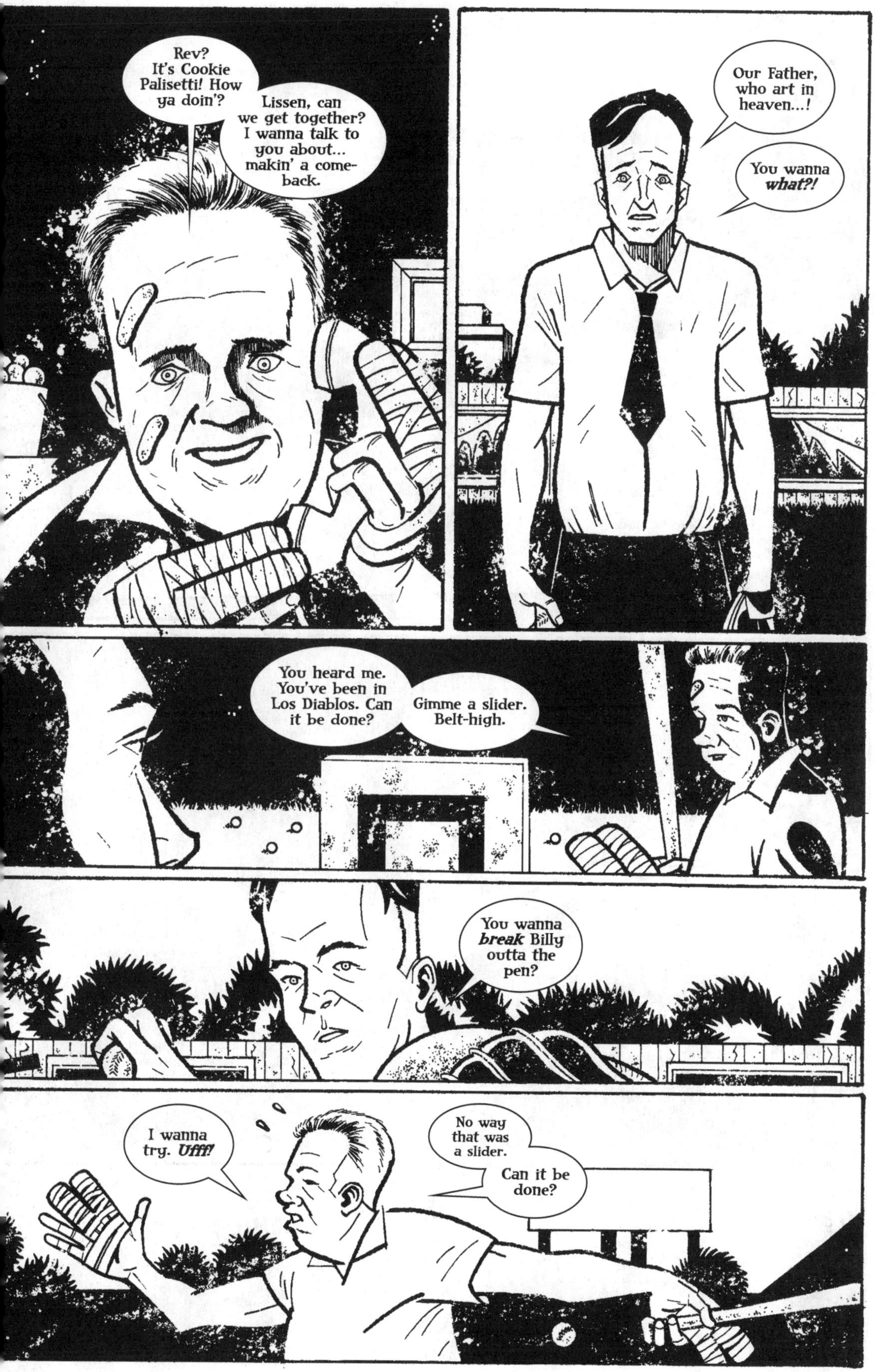
Rev? It's Cookie Palisetti! How ya doin'?
Lissen, can we get together? I wanna talk to you about... makin' a come-back.
Our Father, who art in heaven...!
You wanna *what?!*
You heard me. You've been in Los Diablos. Can it be done?
Gimme a slider. Belt-high.
You wanna *break* Billy outta the pen?
I wanna try. *Ufff!*
No way that was a slider.
Can it be done?

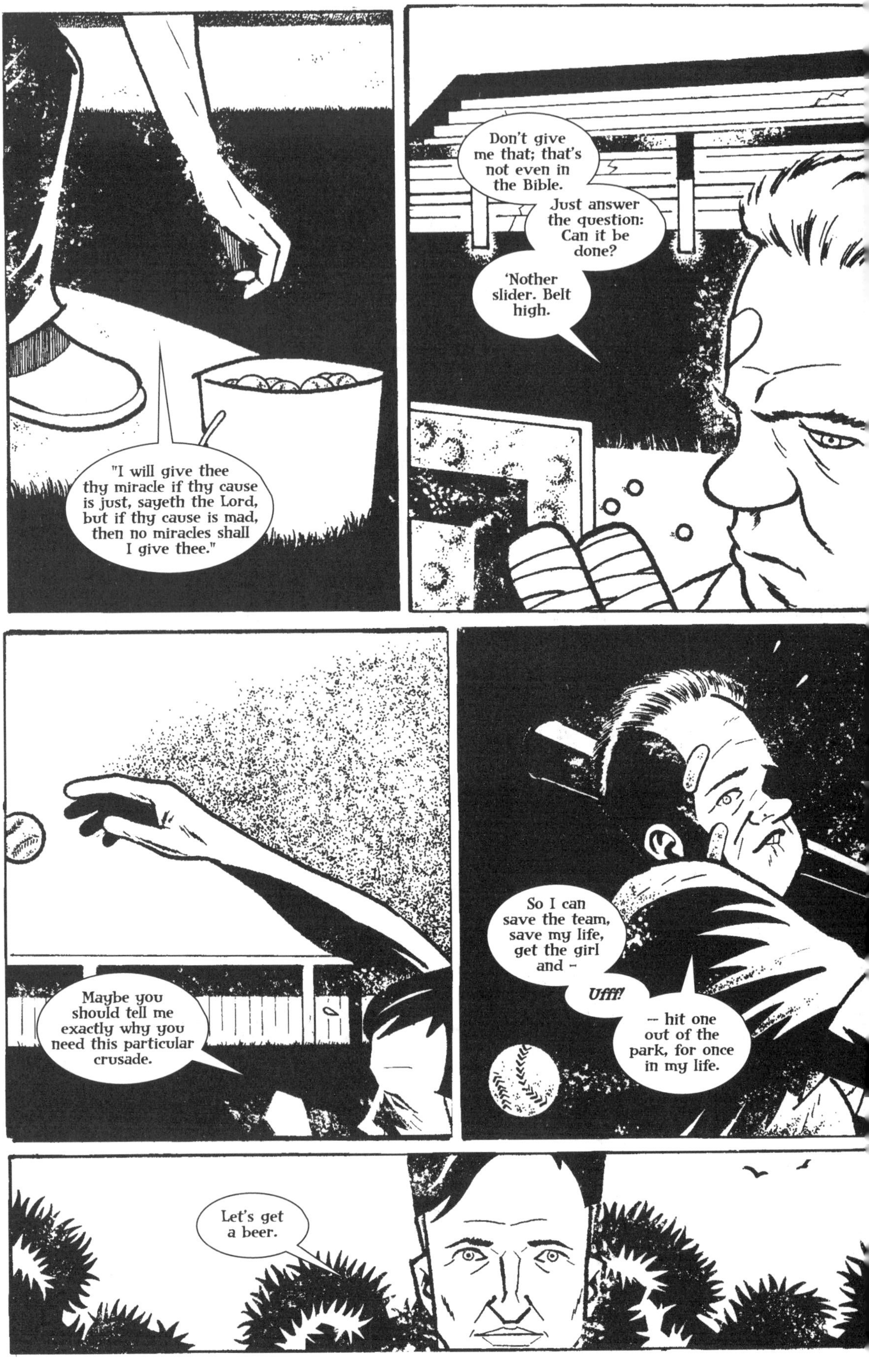
"I will give thee thy miracle if thy cause is just, sayeth the Lord, but if thy cause is mad, then no miracles shall I give thee."
Don't give me that; that's not even in the Bible.
Just answer the question: Can it be done?
'Nother slider. Belt high.
Maybe you should tell me exactly why you need this particular crusade.
So I can save the team, save my life, get the girl and –
Ufff!
-- hit one out of the park, for once in my life.
Let's get a beer.

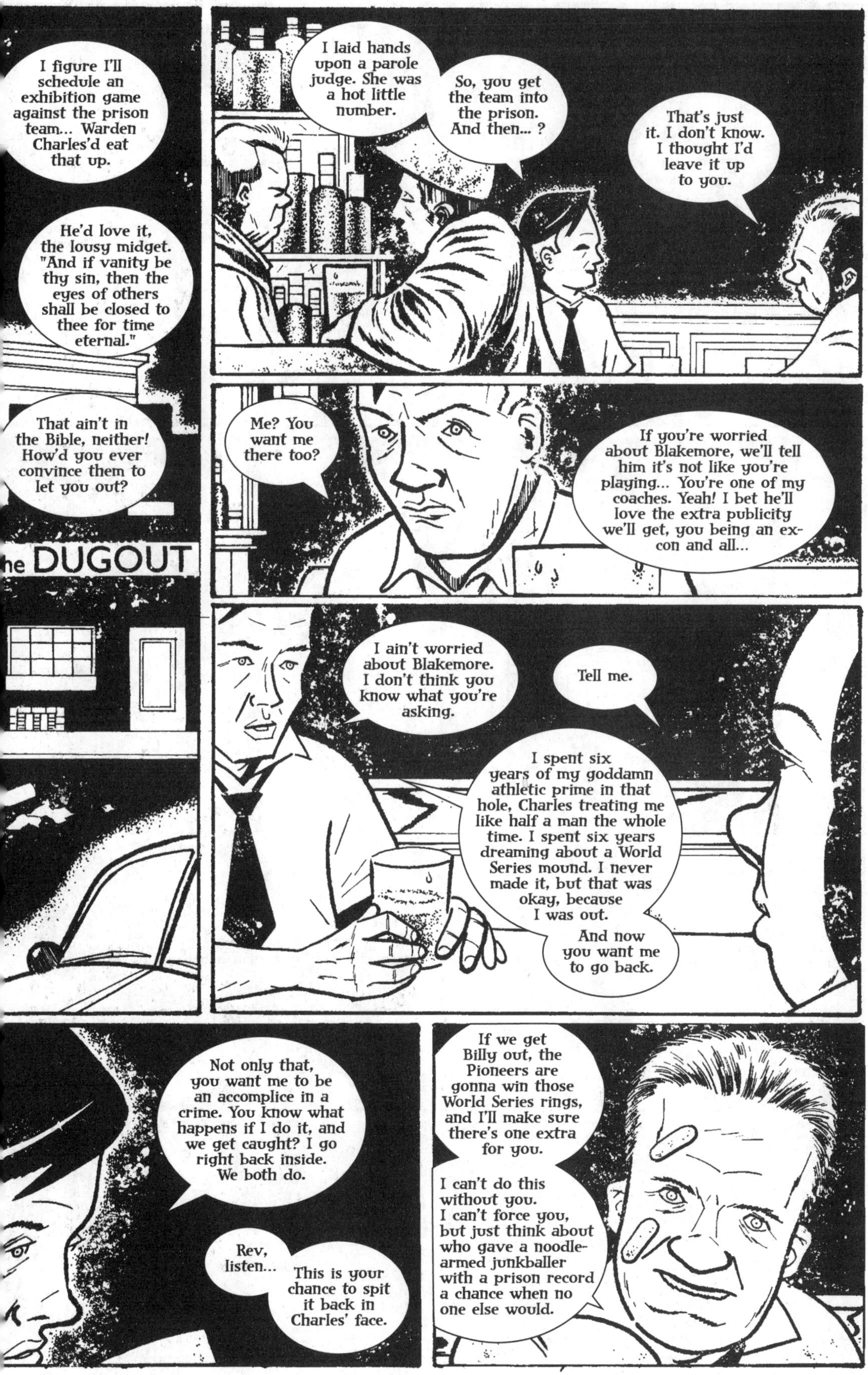
I figure I'll schedule an exhibition game against the prison team... Warden Charles'd eat that up.
He'd love it, the lousy midget. "And if vanity be thy sin, then the eyes of others shall be closed to thee for time eternal."
That ain't in the Bible, neither! How'd you ever convince them to let you out?
he DUGOUT
I laid hands upon a parole judge. She was a hot little number.
So, you get the team into the prison. And then... ?
That's just it. I don't know. I thought I'd leave it up to you.
Me? You want me there too?
If you're worried about Blakemore, we'll tell him it's not like you're playing... You're one of my coaches. Yeah! I bet he'll love the extra publicity we'll get, you being an ex-con and all...
I ain't worried about Blakemore. I don't think you know what you're asking.
Tell me.
I spent six years of my goddamn athletic prime in that hole, Charles treating me like half a man the whole time. I spent six years dreaming about a World Series mound. I never made it, but that was okay, because I was out.
And now you want me to go back.
Not only that, you want me to be an accomplice in a crime. You know what happens if I do it, and we get caught? I go right back inside. We both do.
Rev, listen...
This is your chance to spit it back in Charles' face.
If we get Billy out, the Pioneers are gonna win those World Series rings, and I'll make sure there's one extra for you.
I can't do this without you. I can't force you, but just think about who gave a noodle-armed junkballer with a prison record a chance when no one else would.

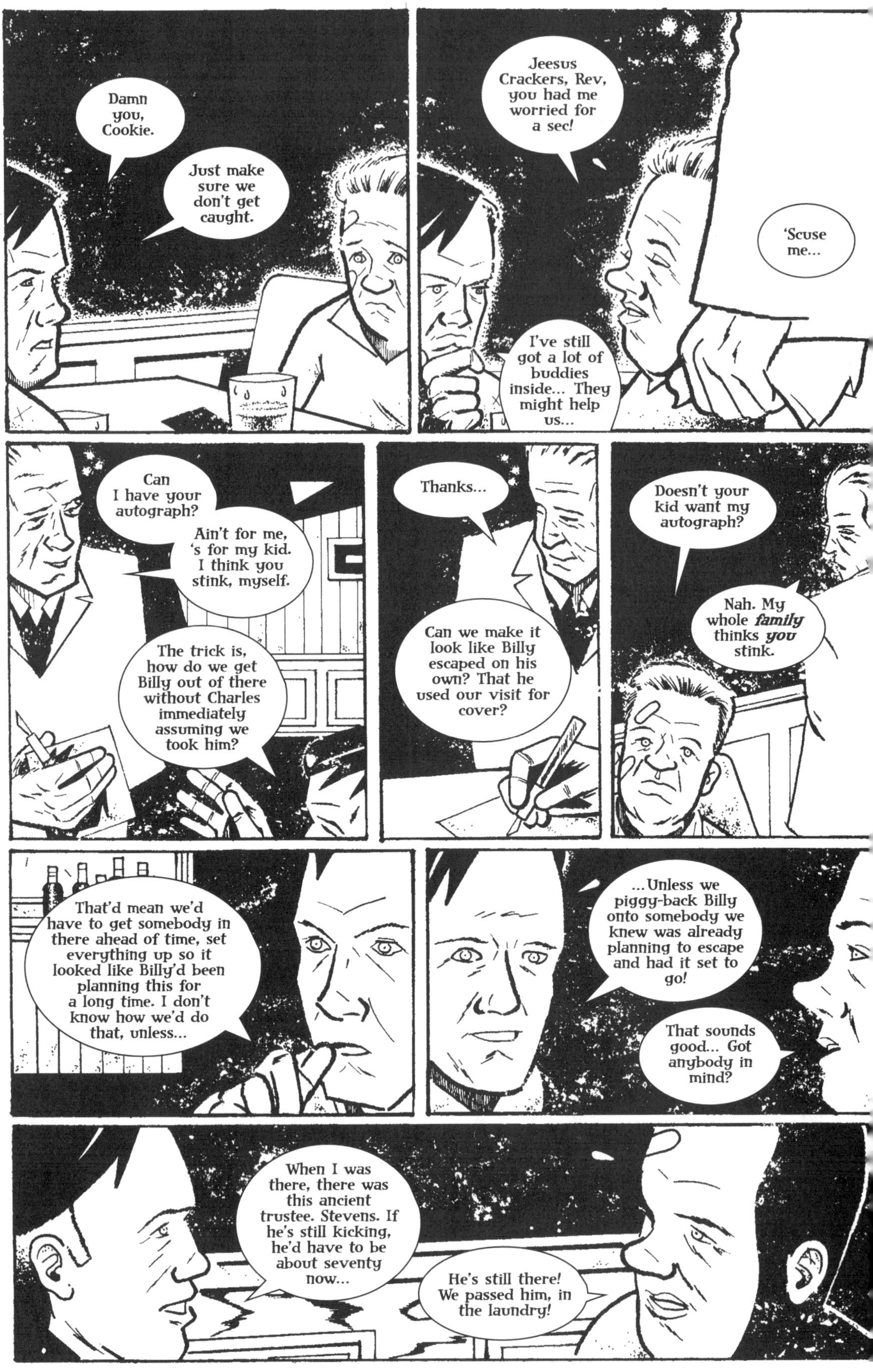
Damn you, Cookie.
Just make sure we don't get caught.
Jeesus Crackers, Rev, you had me worried for a sec!
I've still got a lot of buddies inside... They might help us...
'Scuse me...
Can I have your autograph?
Ain't for me, 's for my kid. I think you stink, myself.
The trick is, how do we get Billy out of there without Charles immediately assuming we took him?
Thanks...
Can we make it look like Billy escaped on his own? That he used our visit for cover?
Doesn't your kid want my autograph?
Nah. My whole *family* thinks *you* stink.
That'd mean we'd have to get somebody in there ahead of time, set everything up so it looked like Billy'd been planning this for a long time. I don't know how we'd do that, unless...
...Unless we piggy-back Billy onto somebody we knew was already planning to escape and had it set to go!
That sounds good... Got anybody in mind?
When I was there, there was this ancient trustee. Stevens. If he's still kicking, he'd have to be about seventy now...
He's still there! We passed him, in the laundry!

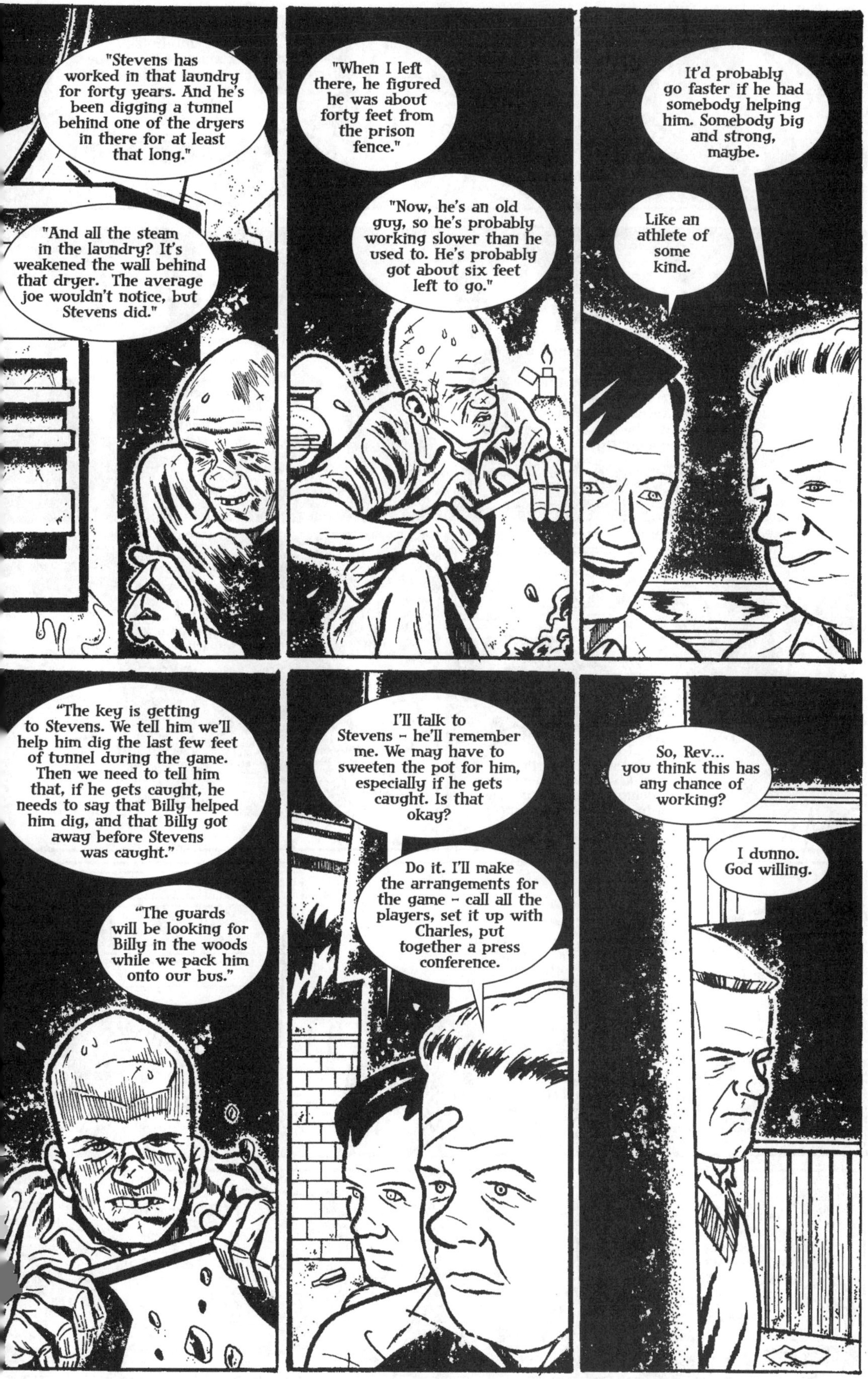
"Stevens has worked in that laundry for forty years. And he's been digging a tunnel behind one of the dryers in there for at least that long."
"And all the steam in the laundry? It's weakened the wall behind that dryer. The average joe wouldn't notice, but Stevens did."
"When I left there, he figured he was about forty feet from the prison fence."
"Now, he's an old guy, so he's probably working slower than he used to. He's probably got about six feet left to go."
It'd probably go faster if he had somebody helping him. Somebody big and strong, maybe.
Like an athlete of some kind.
"The key is getting to Stevens. We tell him we'll help him dig the last few feet of tunnel during the game. Then we need to tell him that, if he gets caught, he needs to say that Billy helped him dig, and that Billy got away before Stevens was caught."
"The guards will be looking for Billy in the woods while we pack him onto our bus."
I'll talk to Stevens – he'll remember me. We may have to sweeten the pot for him, especially if he gets caught. Is that okay?
Do it. I'll make the arrangements for the game – call all the players, set it up with Charles, put together a press conference.
So, Rev... you think this has any chance of working?
I dunno. God willing.

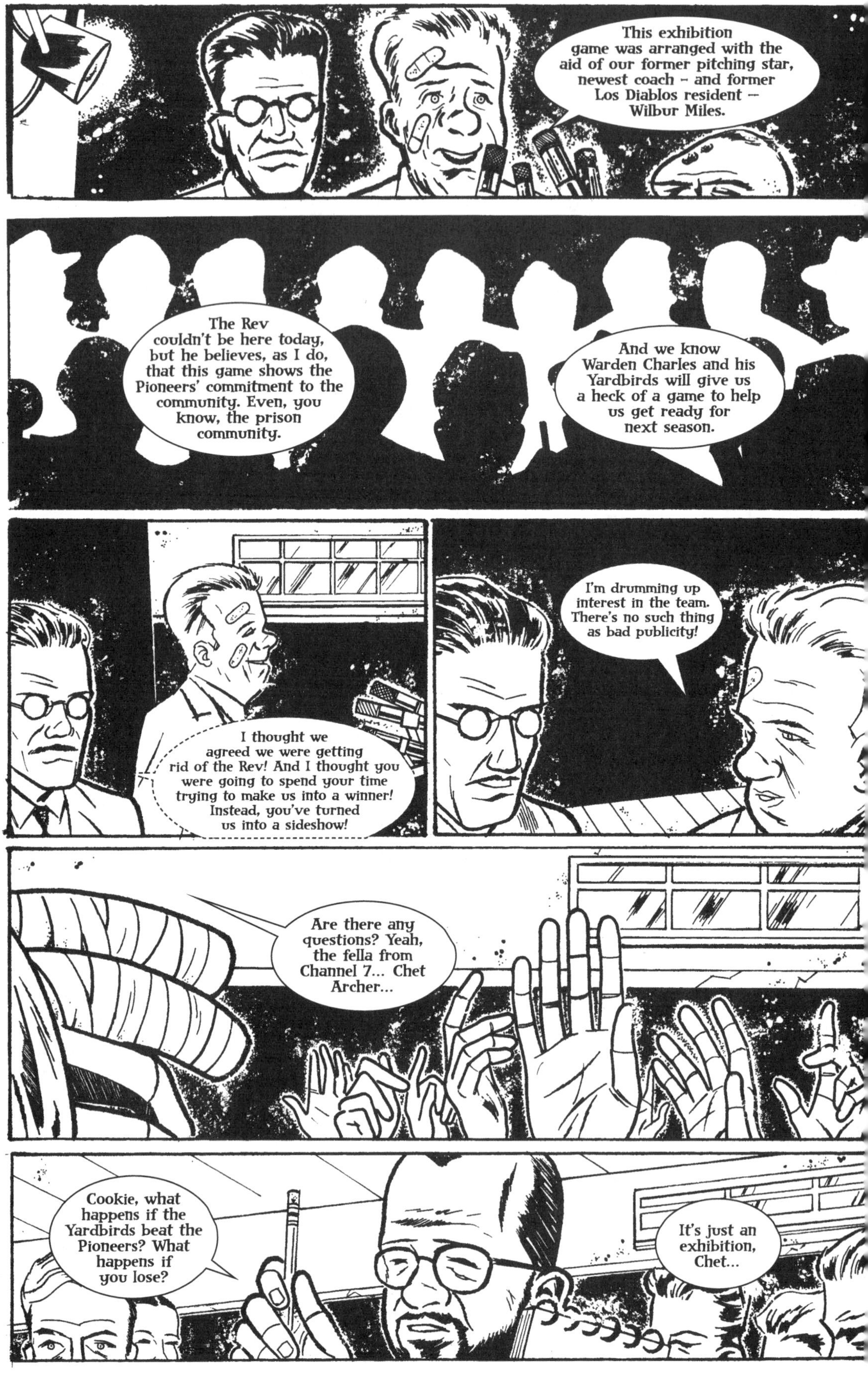
This exhibition game was arranged with the aid of our former pitching star, newest coach – and former Los Diablos resident – Wilbur Miles.
The Rev couldn't be here today, but he believes, as I do, that this game shows the Pioneers' commitment to the community. Even, you know, the prison community.
And we know Warden Charles and his Yardbirds will give us a heck of a game to help us get ready for next season.
I thought we agreed we were getting rid of the Rev! And I thought you were going to spend your time trying to make us into a winner! Instead, you've turned us into a sideshow!
I'm drumming up interest in the team. There's no such thing as bad publicity!
Are there any questions? Yeah, the fella from Channel 7... Chet Archer...
Cookie, what happens if the Yardbirds beat the Pioneers? What happens if you lose?
It's just an exhibition, Chet...

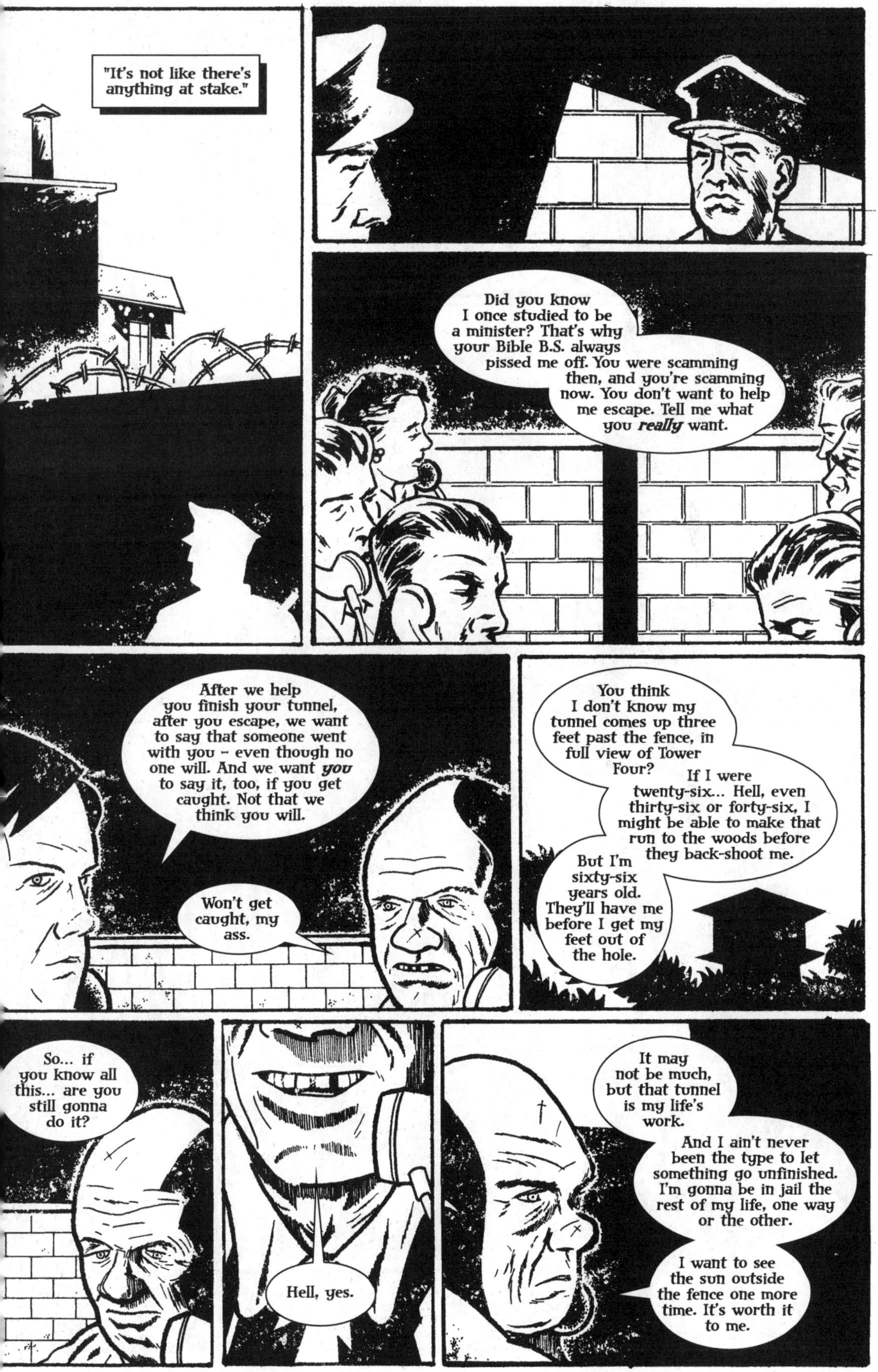

"It's not like there's anything at stake."
Did you know I once studied to be a minister? That's why your Bible B.S. always pissed me off. You were scamming then, and you're scamming now. You don't want to help me escape. Tell me what you *really* want.
After we help you finish your tunnel, after you escape, we want to say that someone went with you - even though no one will. And we want *you* to say it, too, if you get caught. Not that we think you will.
Won't get caught, my ass.
You think I don't know my tunnel comes up three feet past the fence, in full view of Tower Four?
If I were twenty-six... Hell, even thirty-six or forty-six, I might be able to make that run to the woods before they back-shoot me.
But I'm sixty-six years old. They'll have me before I get my feet out of the hole.
So... if you know all this... are you still gonna do it?
Hell, yes.
It may not be much, but that tunnel is my life's work.
And I ain't never been the type to let something go unfinished. I'm gonna be in jail the rest of my life, one way or the other.
I want to see the sun outside the fence one more time. It's worth it to me.

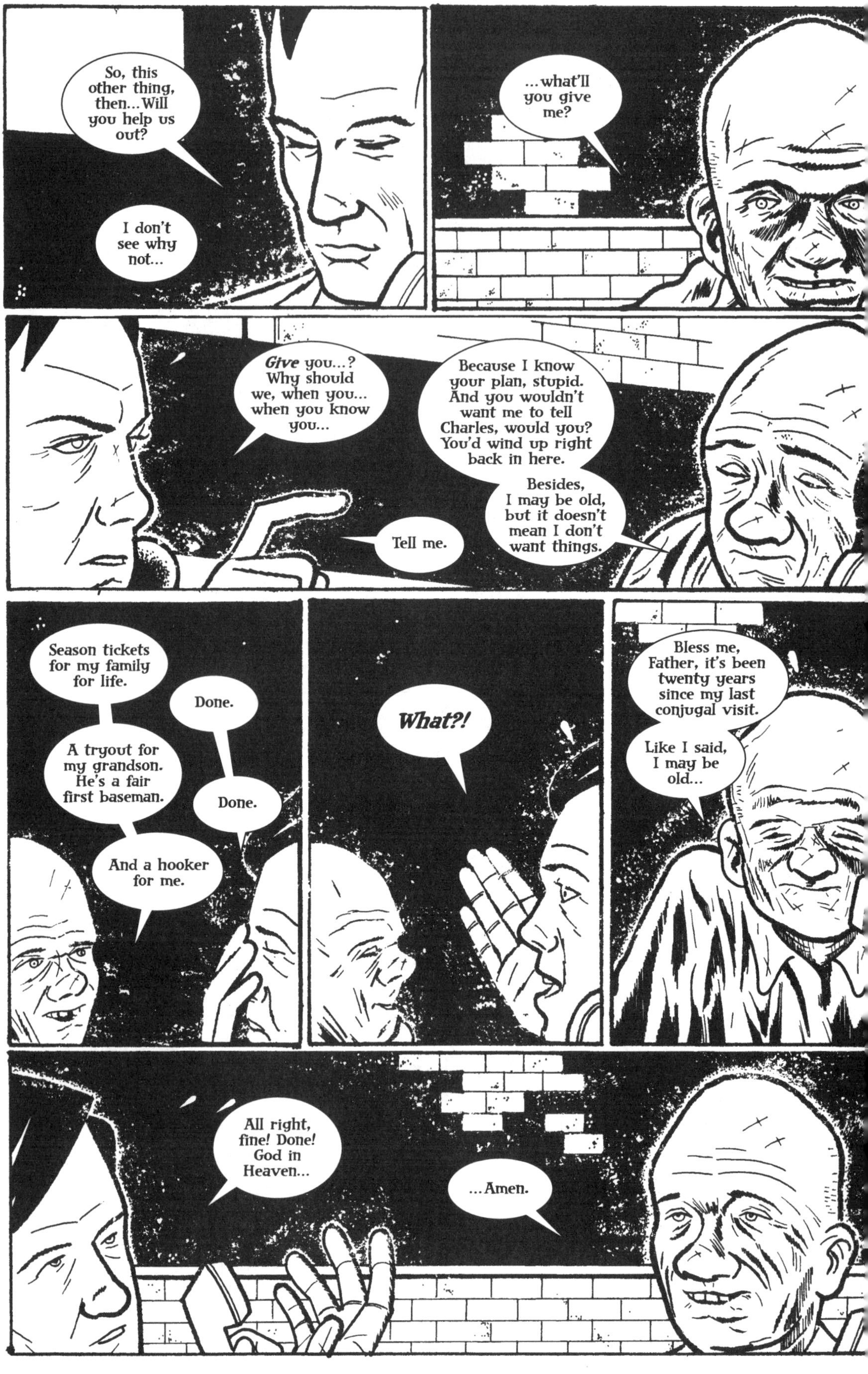
So, this other thing, then...Will you help us out?
I don't see why not...
...what'll you give me?
Give you...? Why should we, when you... when you know you...
Because I know your plan, stupid. And you wouldn't want me to tell Charles, would you? You'd wind up right back in here.
Besides, I may be old, but it doesn't mean I don't want things.
Tell me.
Season tickets for my family for life.
Done.
A tryout for my grandson. He's a fair first baseman.
Done.
And a hooker for me.
What?!
Bless me, Father, it's been twenty years since my last conjugal visit.
Like I said, I may be old...
All right, fine! Done! God in Heaven...
...Amen.

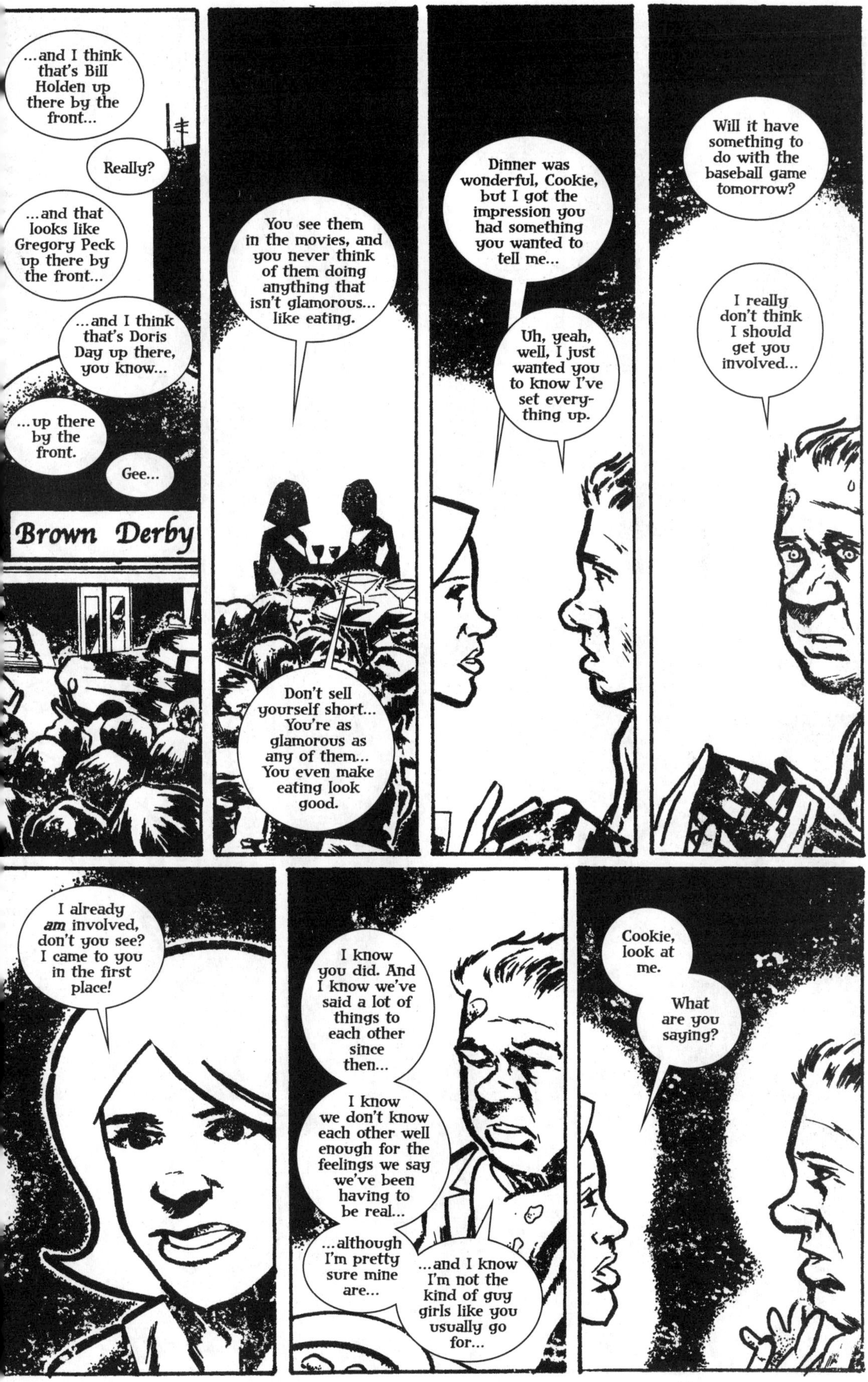
...and I think that's Bill Holden up there by the front...
Really?
...and that looks like Gregory Peck up there by the front...
...and I think that's Doris Day up there, you know...
...up there by the front.
Gee...
Brown Derby
You see them in the movies, and you never think of them doing anything that isn't glamorous... like eating.
Don't sell yourself short... You're as glamorous as any of them... You even make eating look good.
Dinner was wonderful, Cookie, but I got the impression you had something you wanted to tell me...
Uh, yeah, well, I just wanted you to know I've set every-thing up.
Will it have something to do with the baseball game tomorrow?
I really don't think I should get you involved...
I already *am* involved, don't you see? I came to you in the first place!
I know you did. And I know we've said a lot of things to each other since then...
I know we don't know each other well enough for the feelings we say we've been having to be real...
...although I'm pretty sure mine are...
...and I know I'm not the kind of guy girls like you usually go for...
Cookie, look at me.
What are you saying?

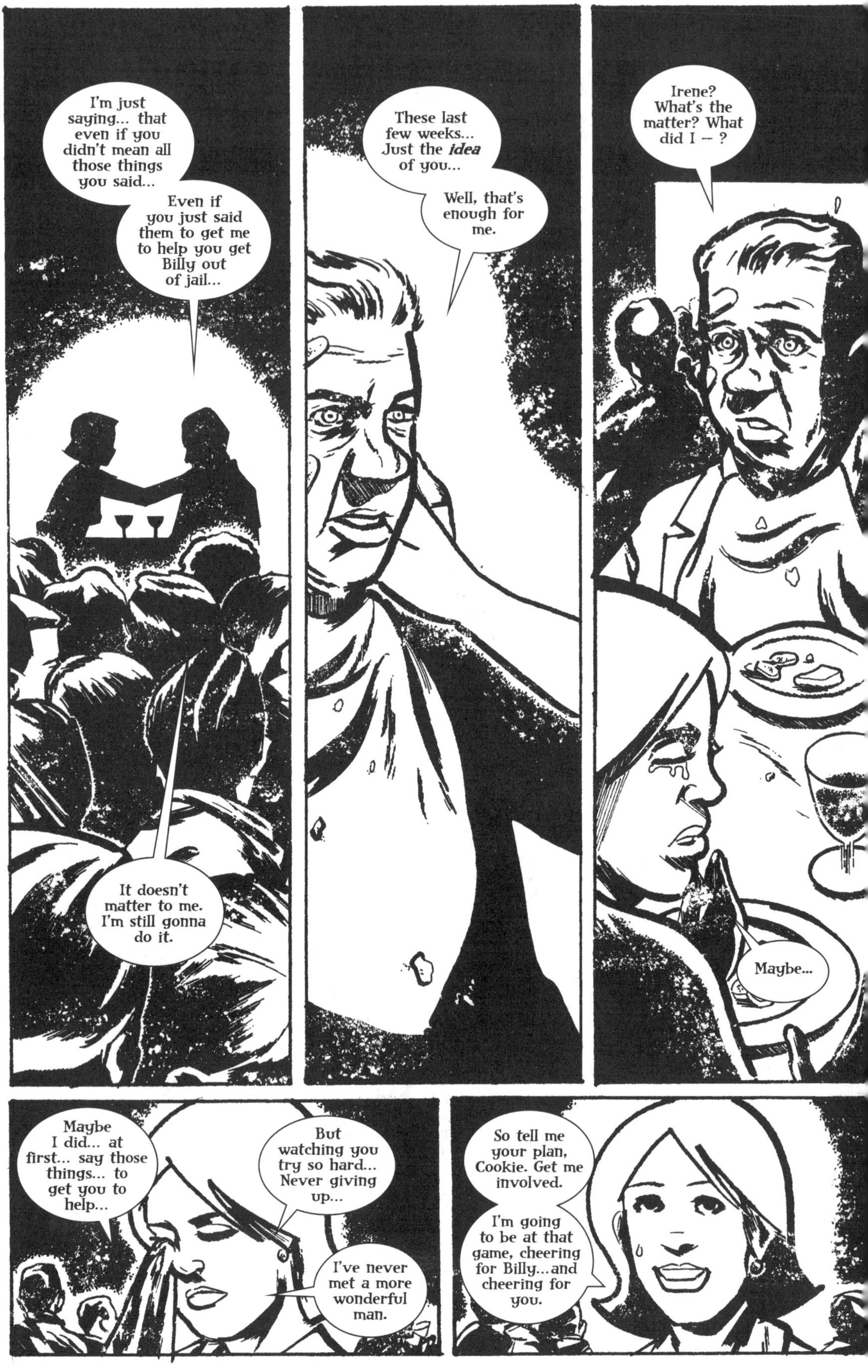
I'm just saying... that even if you didn't mean all those things you said...
Even if you just said them to get me to help you get Billy out of jail...
It doesn't matter to me. I'm still gonna do it.
These last few weeks... Just the *idea* of you...
Well, that's enough for me.
Irene? What's the matter? What did I -- ?
Maybe...
Maybe I did... at first... say those things... to get you to help...
But watching you try so hard... Never giving up...
I've never met a more wonderful man.
So tell me your plan, Cookie. Get me involved.
I'm going to be at that game, cheering for Billy...and cheering for you.

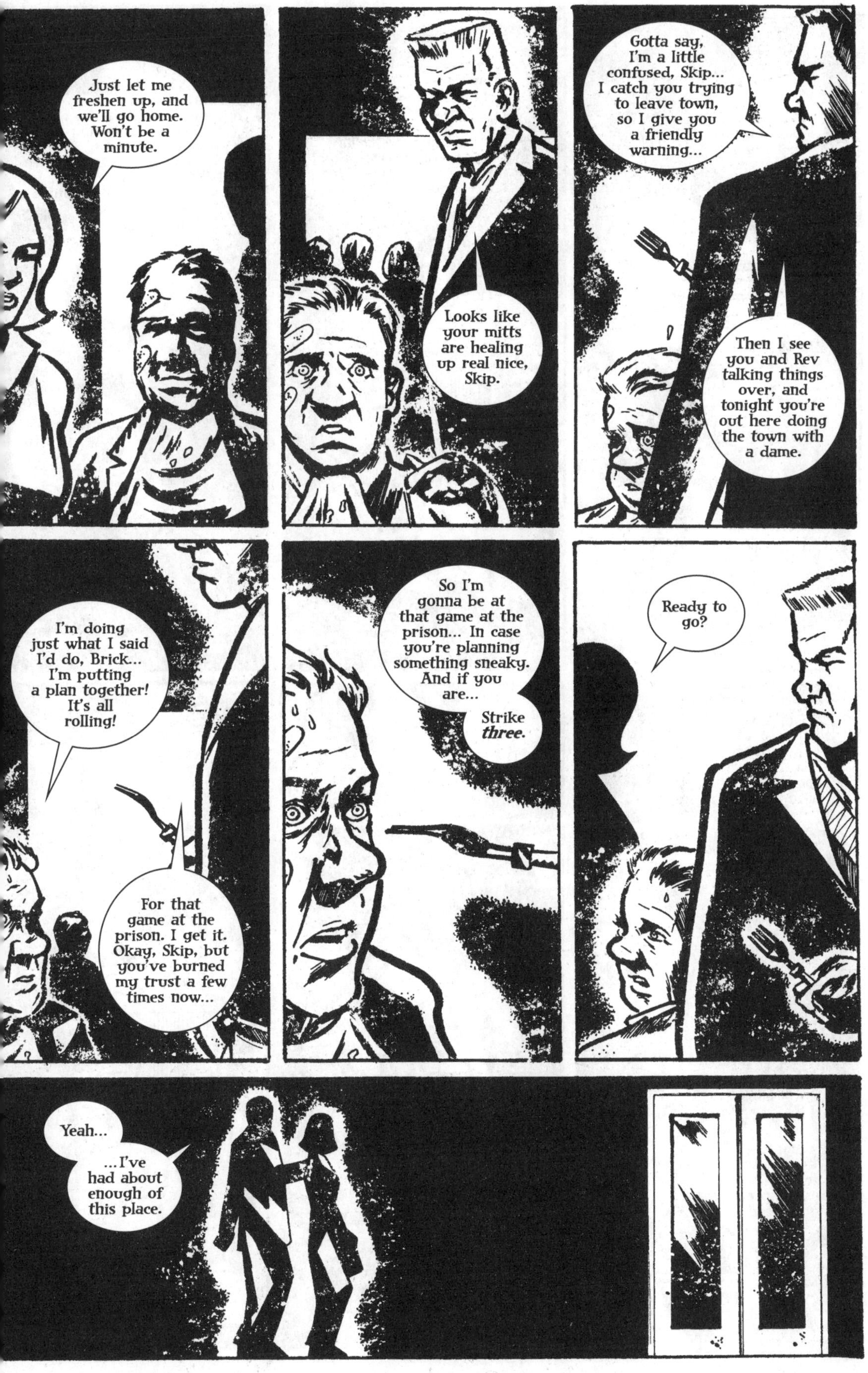
Just let me freshen up, and we'll go home. Won't be a minute.
Looks like your mitts are healing up real nice, Skip.
Gotta say, I'm a little confused, Skip... I catch you trying to leave town, so I give you a friendly warning...
Then I see you and Rev talking things over, and tonight you're out here doing the town with a dame.
I'm doing just what I said I'd do, Brick... I'm putting a plan together! It's all rolling!
For that game at the prison. I get it. Okay, Skip, but you've burned my trust a few times now...
So I'm gonna be at that game at the prison... In case you're planning something sneaky. And if you are...
Strike *three*.
Ready to go?
Yeah...
...I've had about enough of this place.

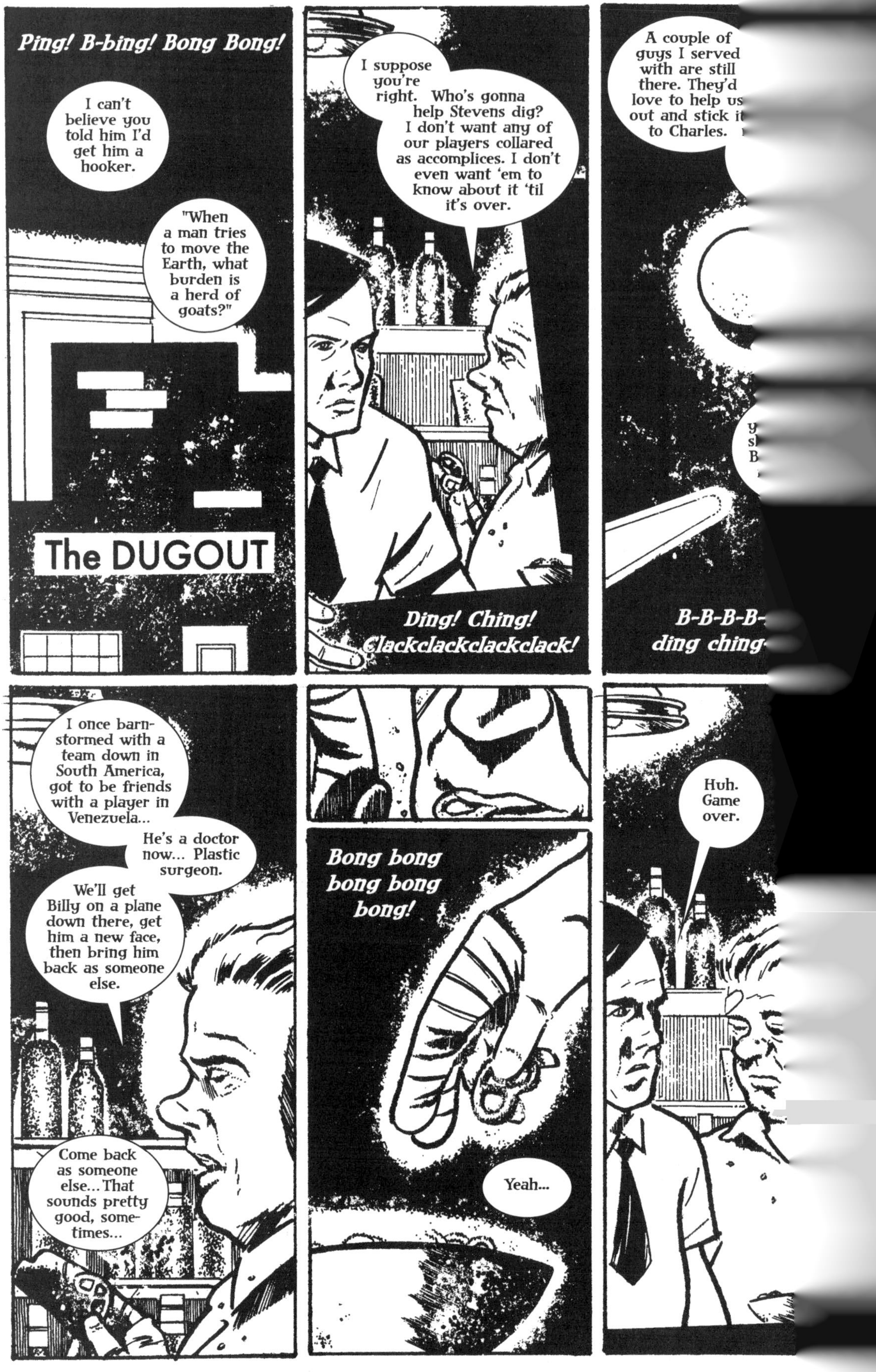
Ping! B-bing! Bong Bong!
I can't believe you told him I'd get him a hooker.
"When a man tries to move the Earth, what burden is a herd of goats?"
The DUGOUT
I suppose you're right. Who's gonna help Stevens dig? I don't want any of our players collared as accomplices. I don't even want 'em to know about it 'til it's over.
Ding! Ching! Clackclackclackclack!
A couple of guys I served with are still there. They'd love to help us out and stick it to Charles.
B-B-B-B-
ding ching-
I once barn-stormed with a team down in South America, got to be friends with a player in Venezuela...
He's a doctor now... Plastic surgeon.
We'll get Billy on a plane down there, get him a new face, then bring him back as someone else.
Come back as someone else... That sounds pretty good, some-times...
Bong bong bong bong bong!
Yeah...
Huh. Game over.

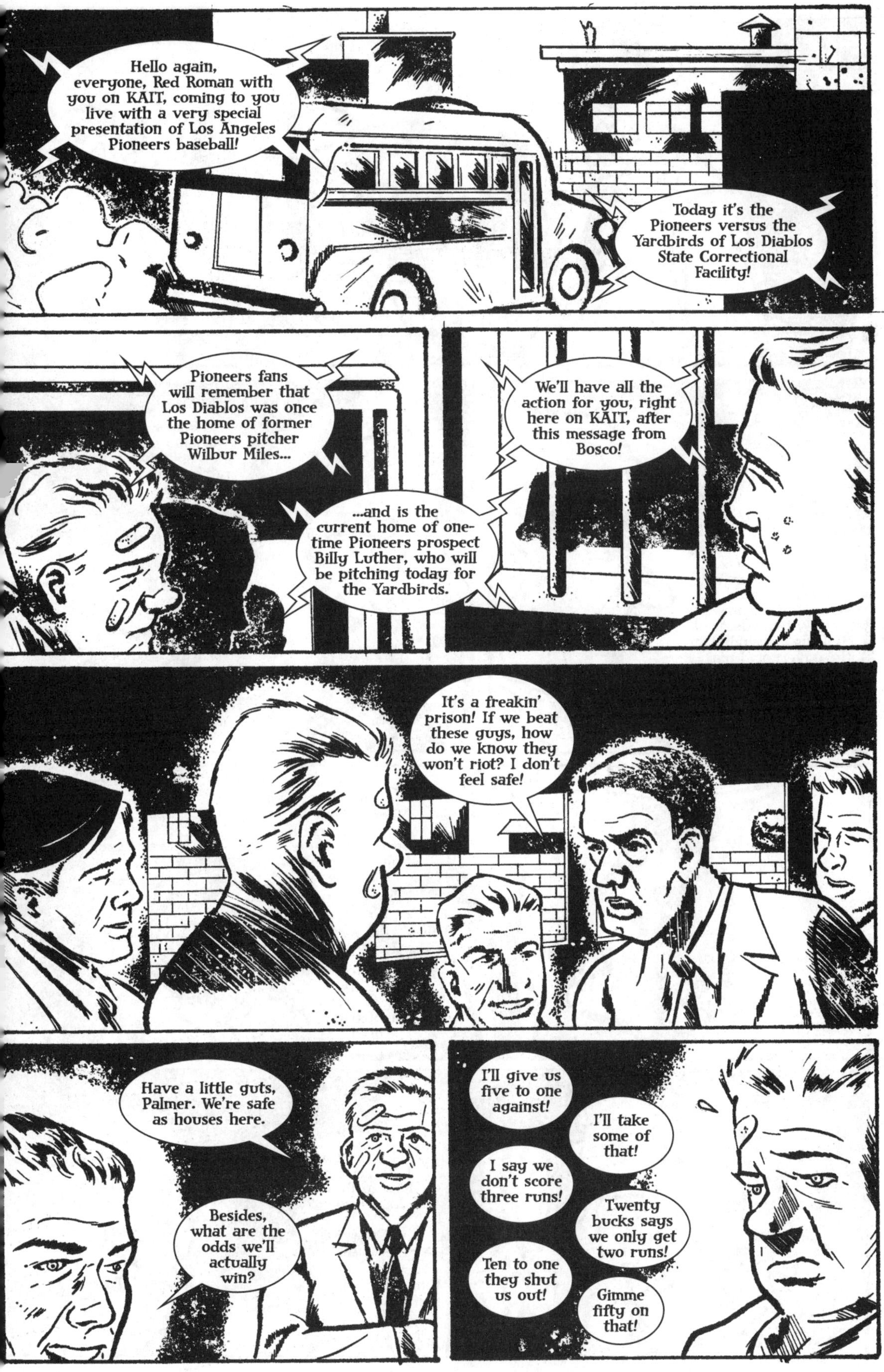
Hello again, everyone, Red Roman with you on KAIT, coming to you live with a very special presentation of Los Angeles Pioneers baseball!
Today it's the Pioneers versus the Yardbirds of Los Diablos State Correctional Facility!
Pioneers fans will remember that Los Diablos was once the home of former Pioneers pitcher Wilbur Miles...
...and is the current home of one-time Pioneers prospect Billy Luther, who will be pitching today for the Yardbirds.
We'll have all the action for you, right here on KAIT, after this message from Bosco!
It's a freakin' prison! If we beat these guys, how do we know they won't riot? I don't feel safe!
Have a little guts, Palmer. We're safe as houses here.
Besides, what are the odds we'll actually win?
I'll give us five to one against!
I'll take some of that!
I say we don't score three runs!
Twenty bucks says we only get two runs!
Ten to one they shut us out!
Gimme fifty on that!

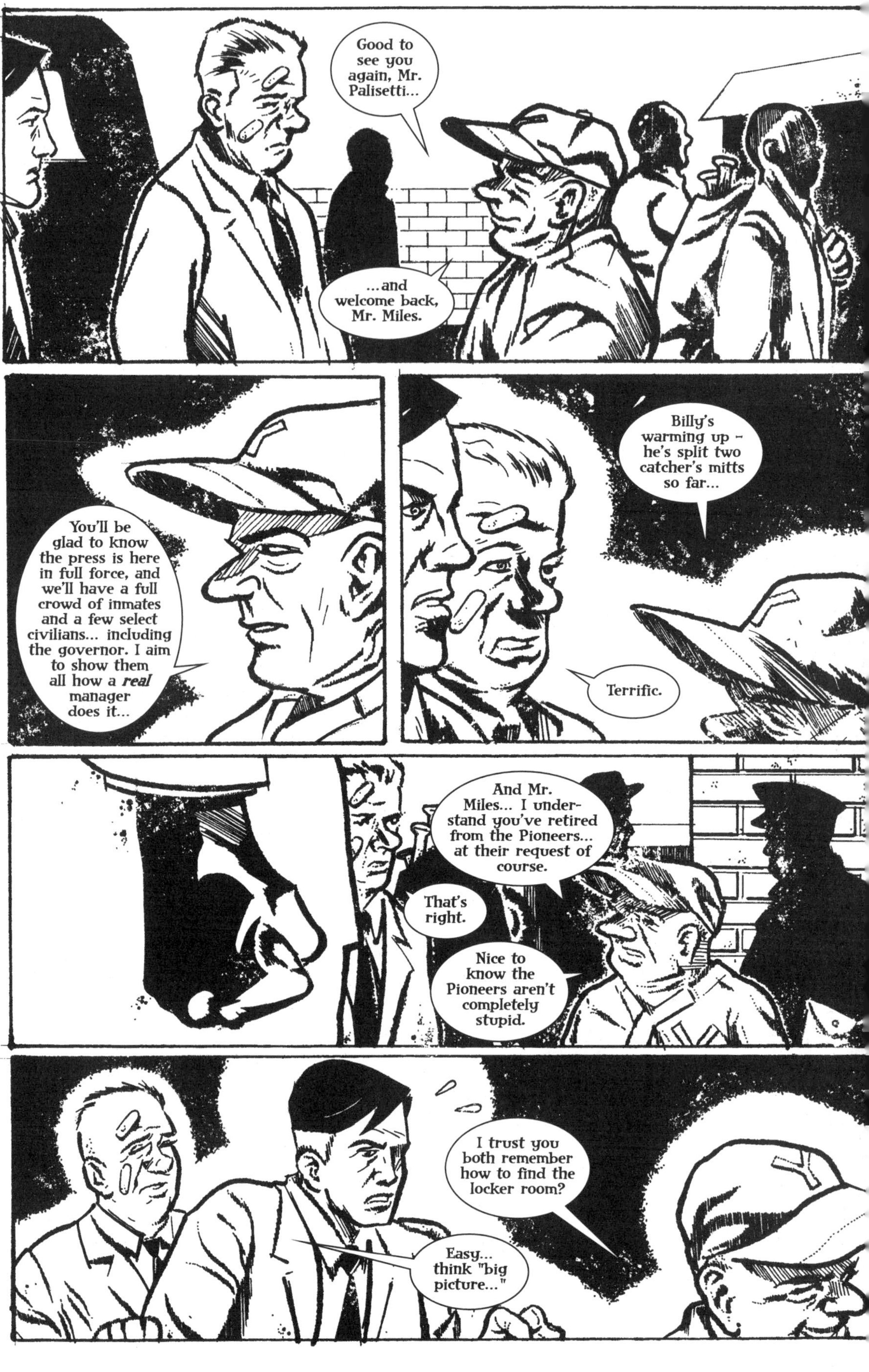
Good to see you again, Mr. Palisetti...
...and welcome back, Mr. Miles.
You'll be glad to know the press is here in full force, and we'll have a full crowd of inmates and a few select civilians... including the governor. I aim to show them all how a *real* manager does it...
Billy's warming up – he's split two catcher's mitts so far...
Terrific.
And Mr. Miles... I understand you've retired from the Pioneers... at their request of course.
That's right.
Nice to know the Pioneers aren't completely stupid.
I trust you both remember how to find the locker room?
Easy... think "big picture..."

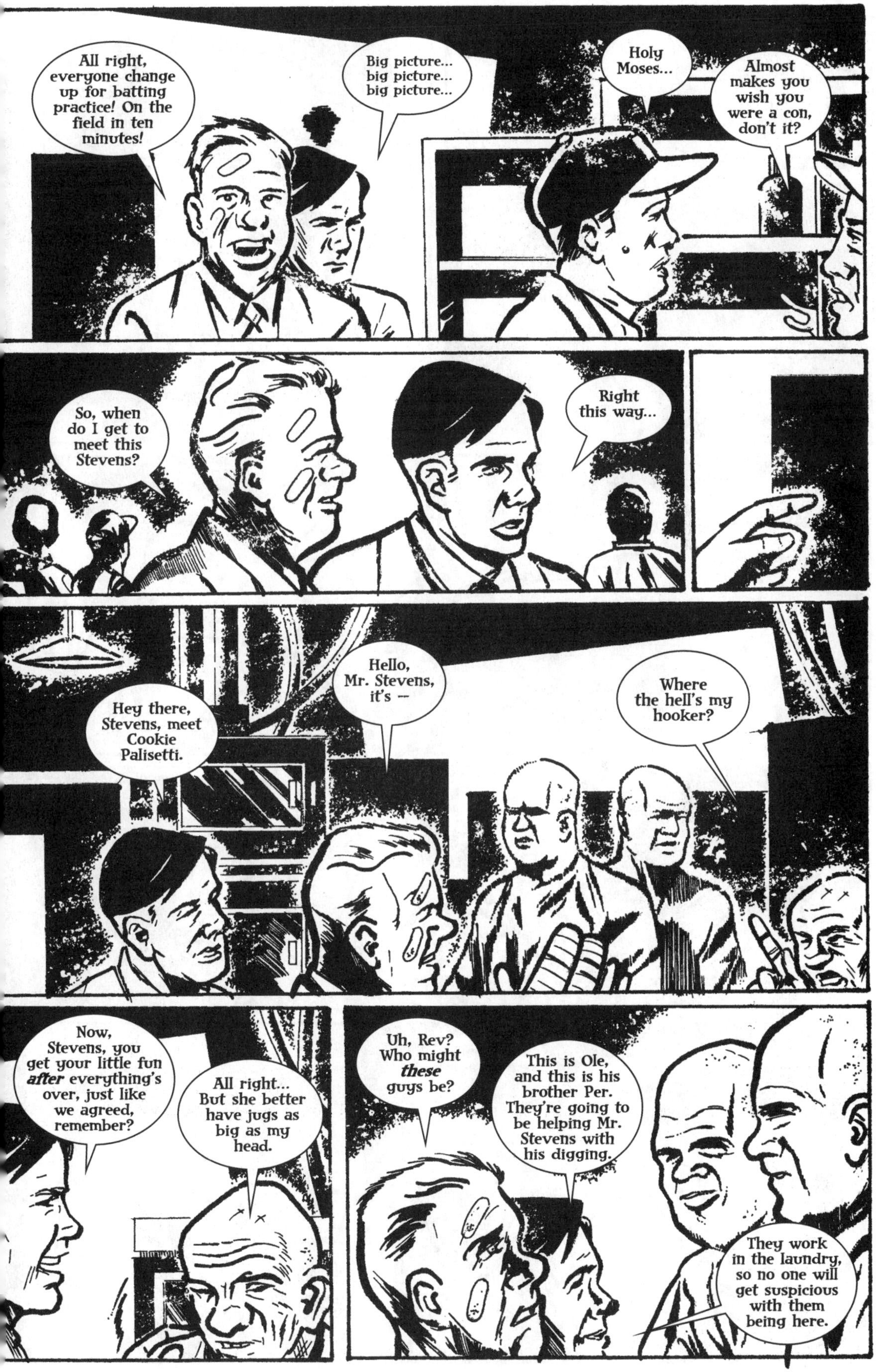
All right, everyone change up for batting practice! On the field in ten minutes!
Big picture... big picture... big picture...
Holy Moses...
Almost makes you wish you were a con, don't it?
So, when do I get to meet this Stevens?
Right this way...
Hey there, Stevens, meet Cookie Palisetti.
Hello, Mr. Stevens, it's --
Where the hell's my hooker?
Now, Stevens, you get your little fun *after* everything's over, just like we agreed, remember?
All right... But she better have jugs as big as my head.
Uh, Rev? Who might *these* guys be?
This is Ole, and this is his brother Per. They're going to be helping Mr. Stevens with his digging.
They work in the laundry, so no one will get suspicious with them being here.

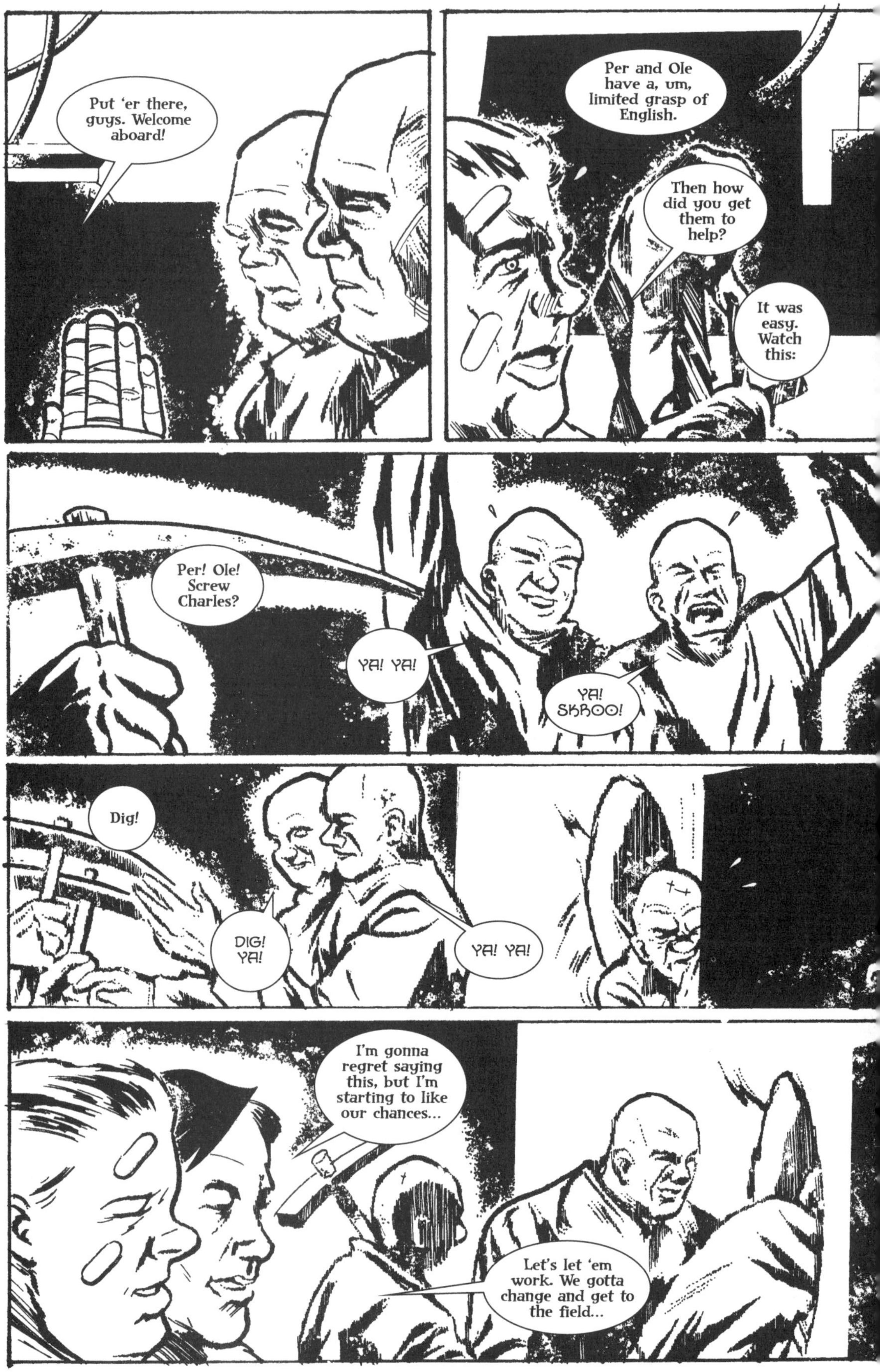
Put 'er there, guys. Welcome aboard!
Per and Ole have a, um, limited grasp of English.
Then how did you get them to help?
It was easy. Watch this:
Per! Ole! Screw Charles?
YA! YA!
YA! SKROO!
Dig!
DIG! YA!
YA! YA!
I'm gonna regret saying this, but I'm starting to like our chances...
Let's let 'em work. We gotta change and get to the field...

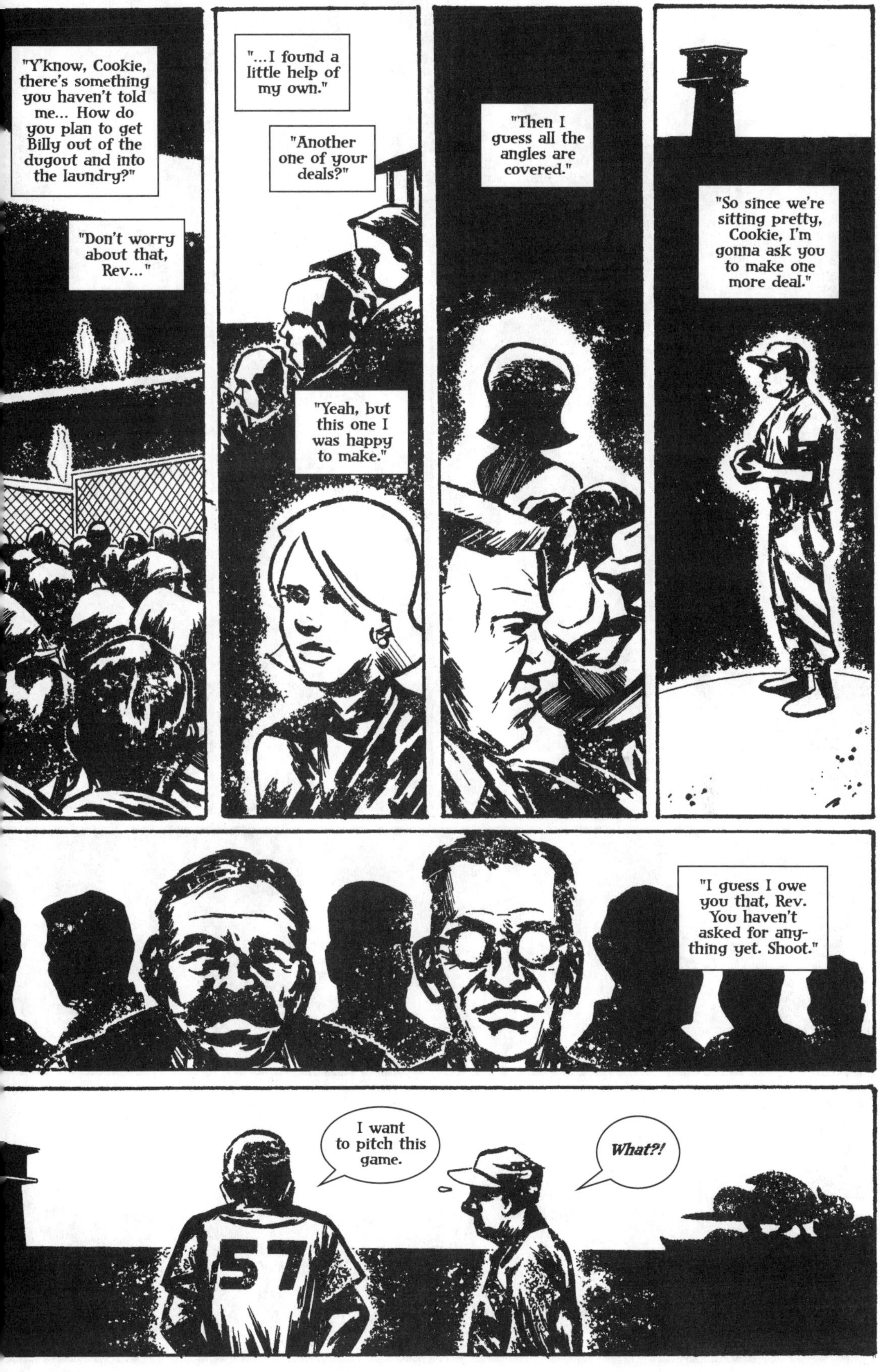
"Y'know, Cookie, there's something you haven't told me... How do you plan to get Billy out of the dugout and into the laundry?"
"Don't worry about that, Rev..."
"...I found a little help of my own."
"Another one of your deals?"
"Yeah, but this one I was happy to make."
"Then I guess all the angles are covered."
"So since we're sitting pretty, Cookie, I'm gonna ask you to make one more deal."
"I guess I owe you that, Rev. You haven't asked for anything yet. Shoot."
I want to pitch this game.
What?!
57

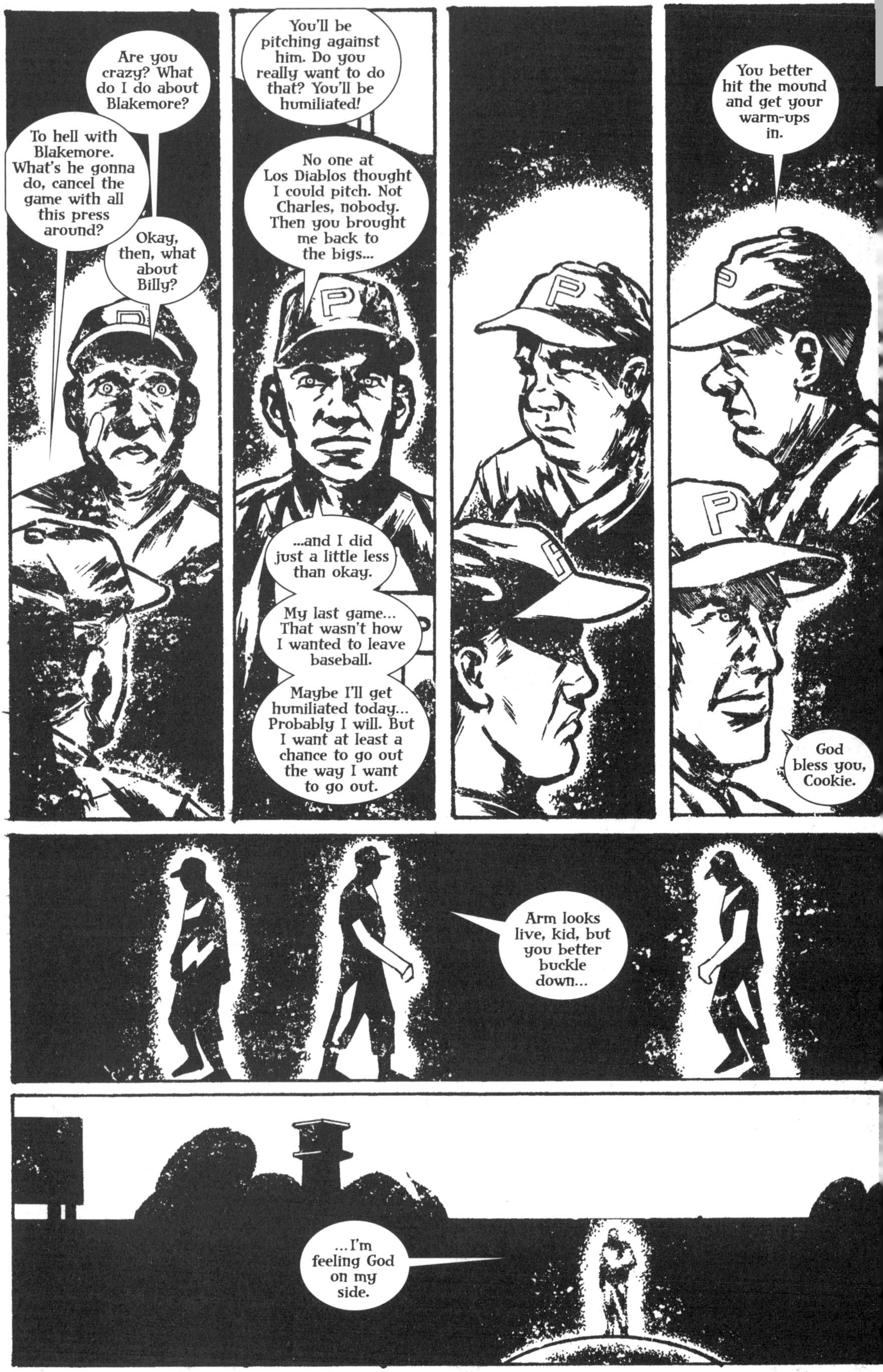
Are you crazy? What do I do about Blakemore?
To hell with Blakemore. What's he gonna do, cancel the game with all this press around?
Okay, then, what about Billy?
You'll be pitching against him. Do you really want to do that? You'll be humiliated!
No one at Los Diablos thought I could pitch. Not Charles, nobody. Then you brought me back to the bigs...
...and I did just a little less than okay.
My last game... That wasn't how I wanted to leave baseball.
Maybe I'll get humiliated today... Probably I will. But I want at least a chance to go out the way I want to go out.
You better hit the mound and get your warm-ups in.
God bless you, Cookie.
Arm looks live, kid, but you better buckle down...
...I'm feeling God on my side.

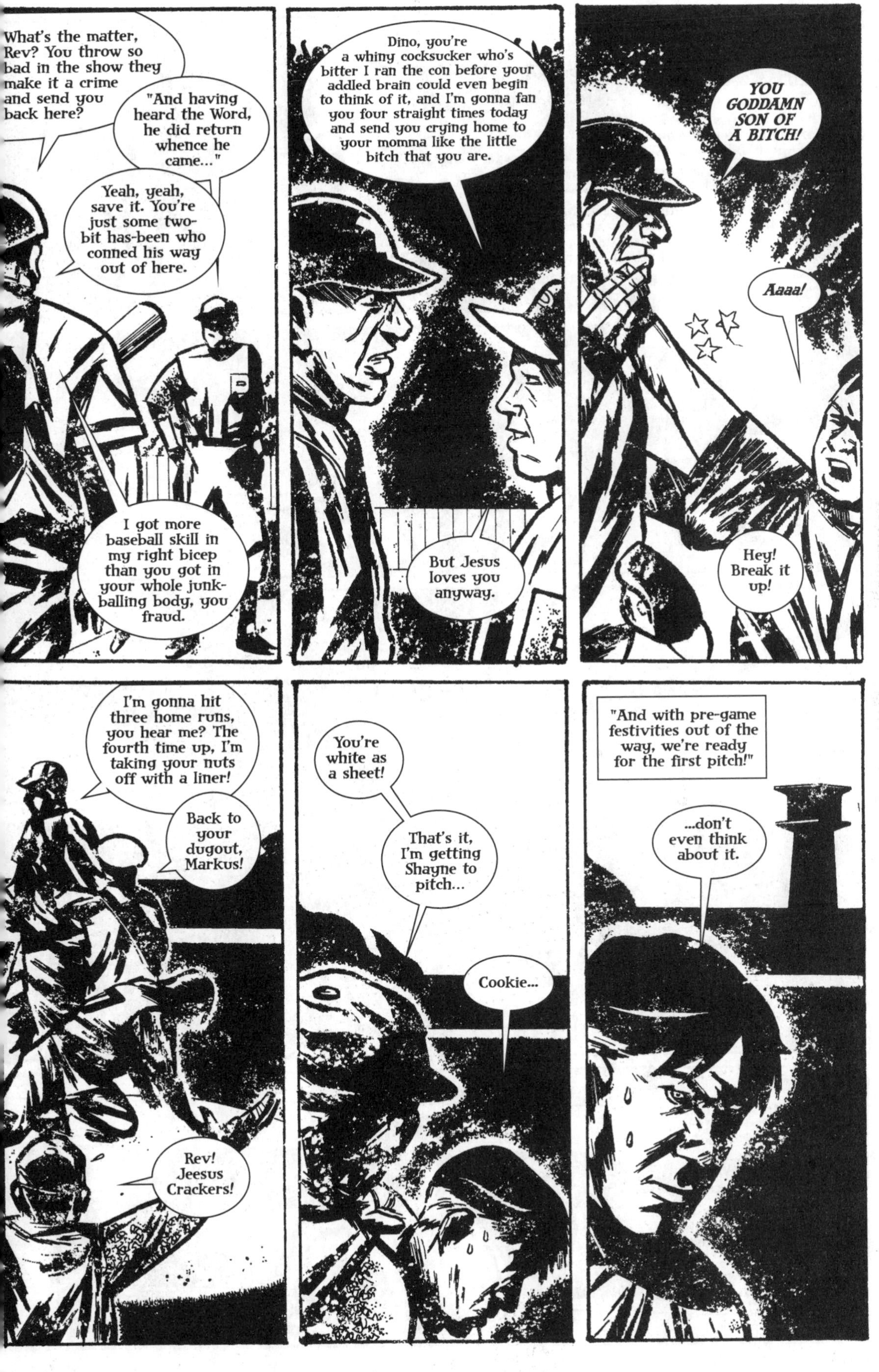
What's the matter, Rev? You throw so bad in the show they make it a crime and send you back here?
"And having heard the Word, he did return whence he came..."
Yeah, yeah, save it. You're just some two-bit has-been who conned his way out of here.
I got more baseball skill in my right bicep than you got in your whole junk-balling body, you fraud.
Dino, you're a whiny cocksucker who's bitter I ran the con before your addled brain could even begin to think of it, and I'm gonna fan you four straight times today and send you crying home to your momma like the little bitch that you are.
But Jesus loves you anyway.
YOU GODDAMN SON OF A BITCH!
Aaaa!
Hey! Break it up!
I'm gonna hit three home runs, you hear me? The fourth time up, I'm taking your nuts off with a liner!
Back to your dugout, Markus!
Rev! Jeesus Crackers!
You're white as a sheet!
That's it, I'm getting Shayne to pitch...
Cookie...
"And with pre-game festivities out of the way, we're ready for the first pitch!"
...don't even think about it.

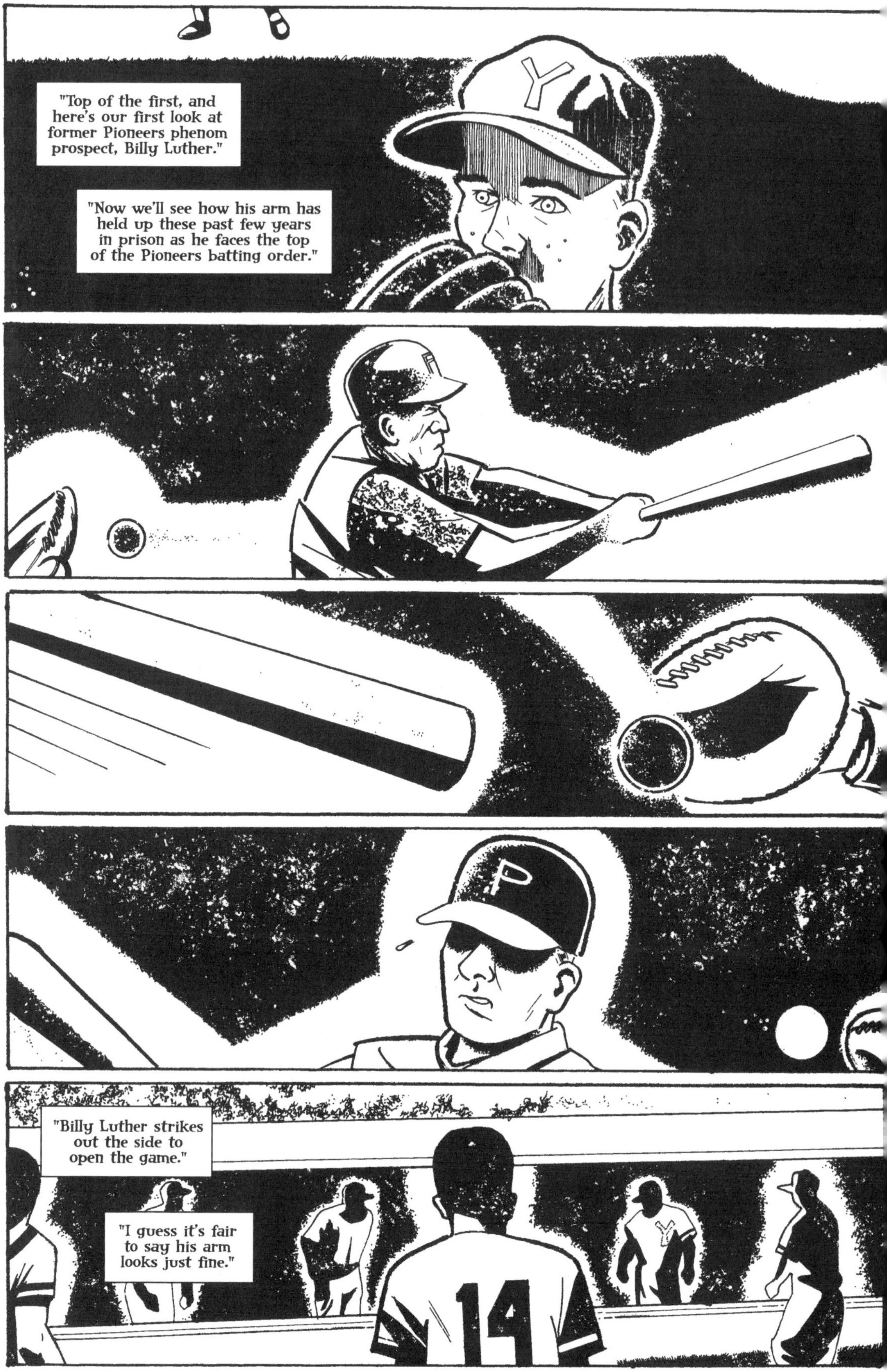
"Top of the first, and here's our first look at former Pioneers phenom prospect, Billy Luther."
"Now we'll see how his arm has held up these past few years in prison as he faces the top of the Pioneers batting order."
"Billy Luther strikes out the side to open the game."
"I guess it's fair to say his arm looks just fine."

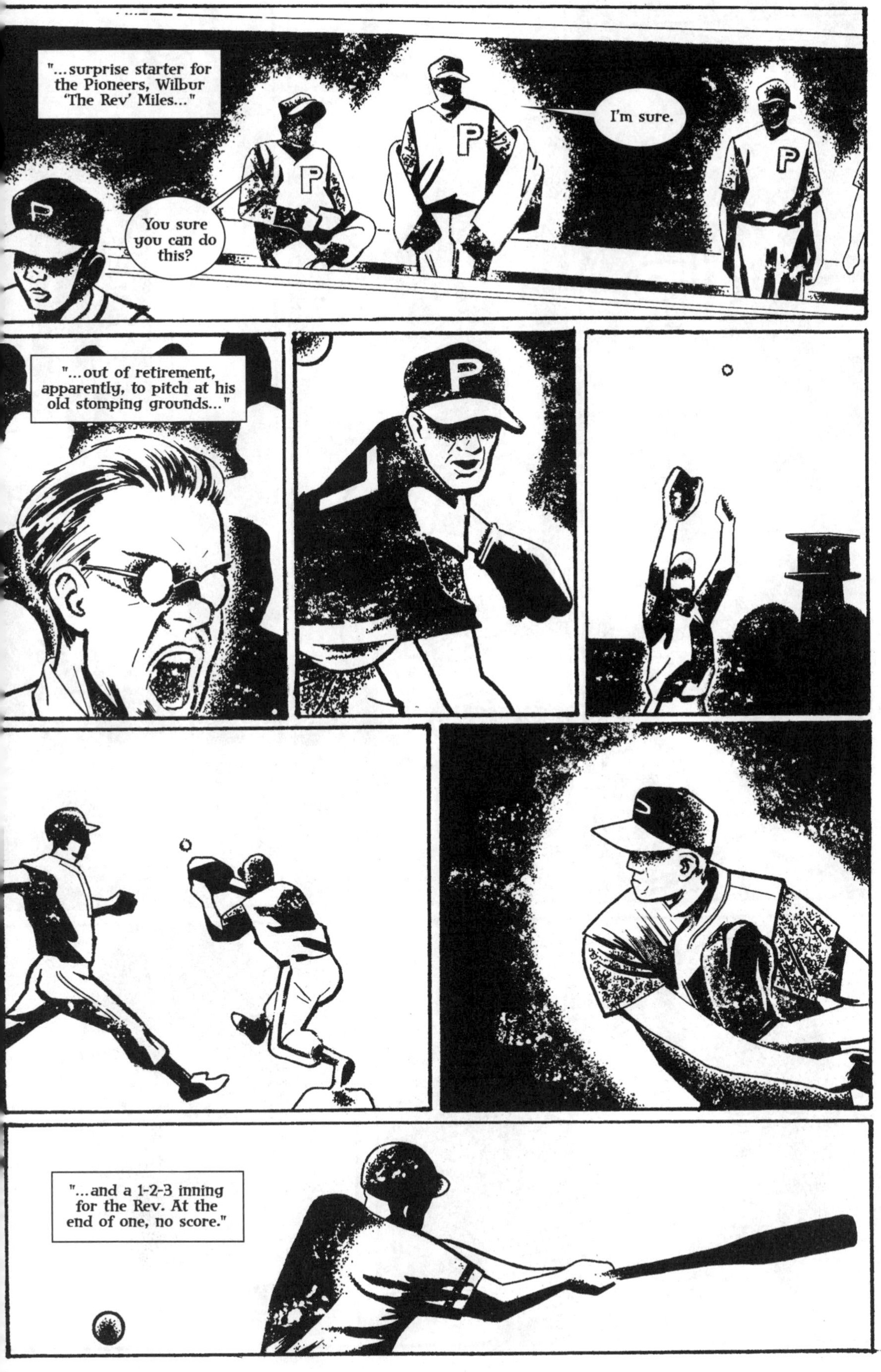
"...surprise starter for the Pioneers, Wilbur 'The Rev' Miles..."
You sure you can do this?
I'm sure.
"...out of retirement, apparently, to pitch at his old stomping grounds..."
"...and a 1-2-3 inning for the Rev. At the end of one, no score."

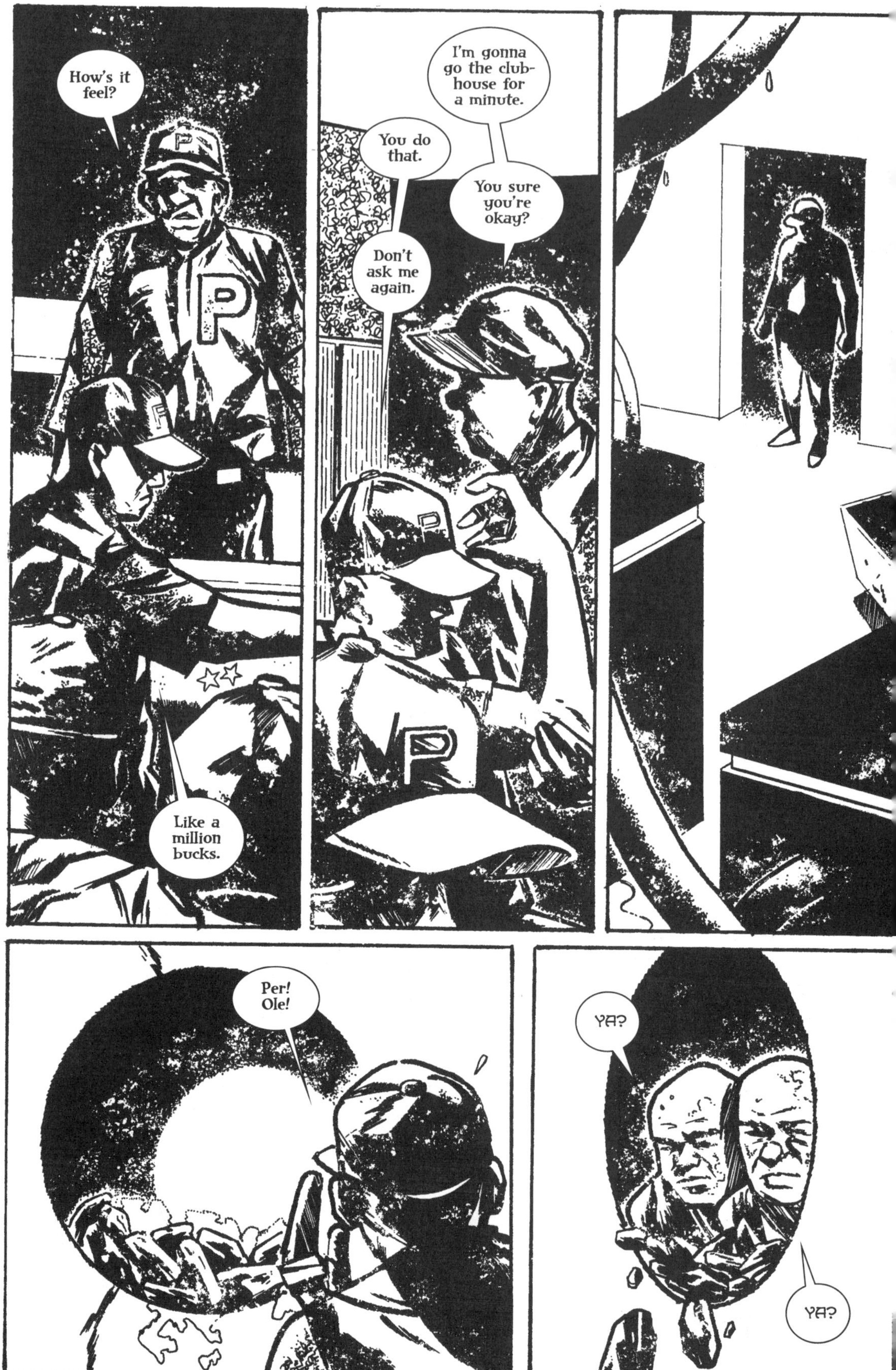
How's it feel?
Like a million bucks.
I'm gonna go the club-house for a minute.
You do that.
You sure you're okay?
Don't ask me again.
Per! Ole!
YA?
YA?

How's it going in there?
Umm...
Uh, dig good?
AH! YA, YA, DIG GOOD!
DIG GOOD! DONE SOON!
DONE DIG SOON!
SKROO CHARLES!

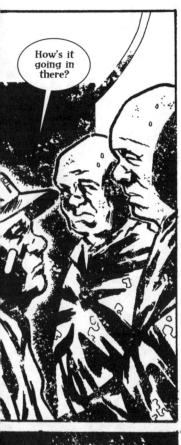

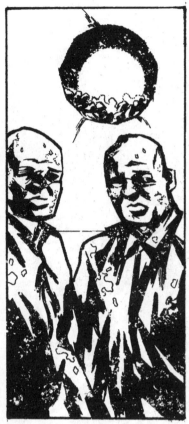

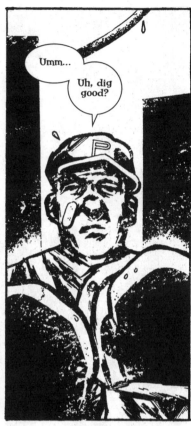

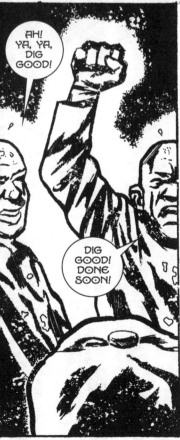

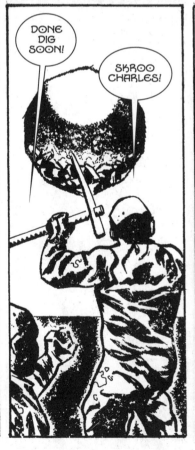

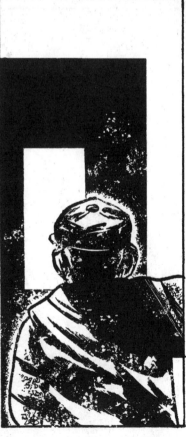

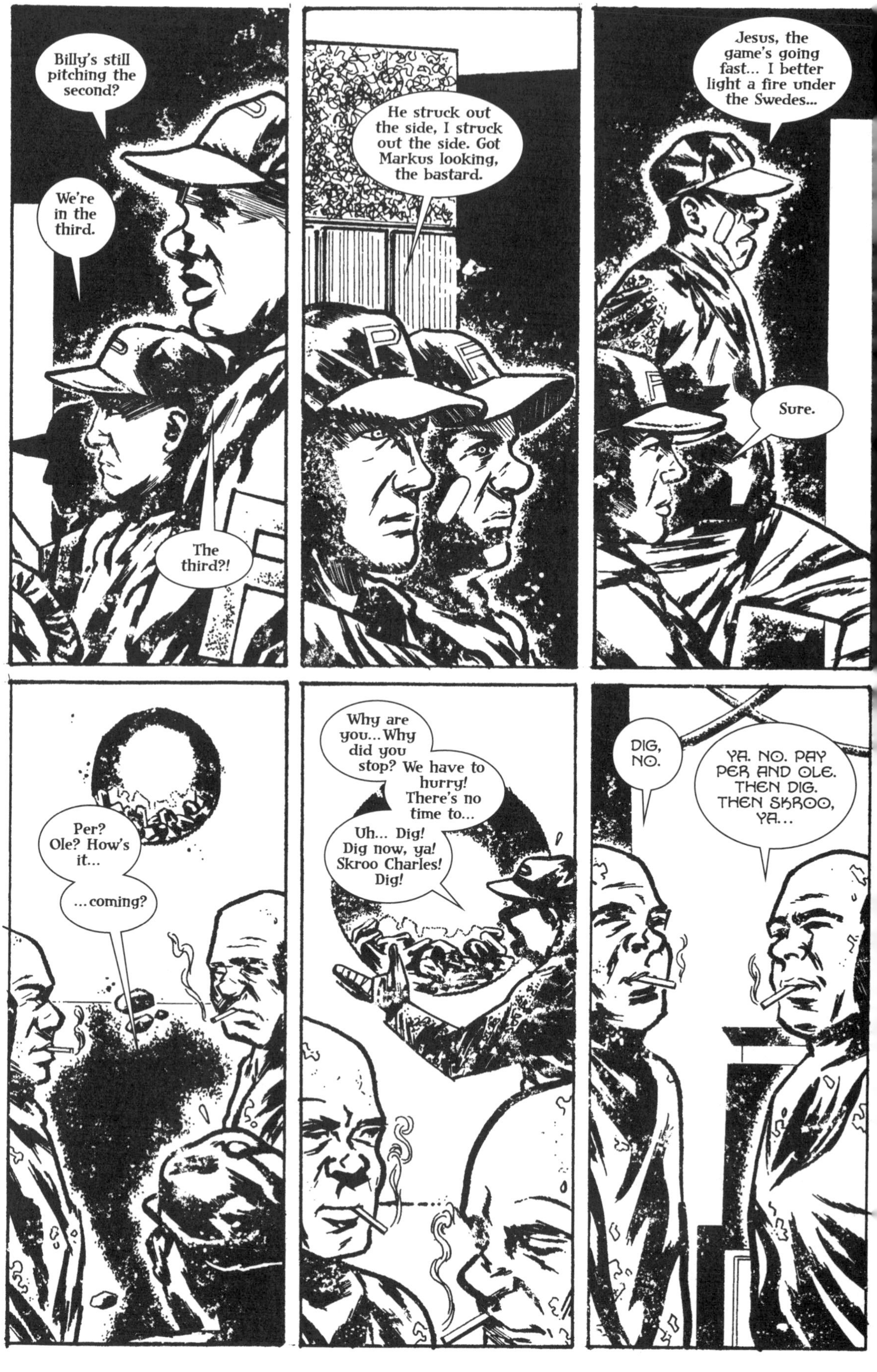
Billy's still pitching the second?
We're in the third.
The third?!
He struck out the side, I struck out the side. Got Markus looking, the bastard.
Jesus, the game's going fast... I better light a fire under the Swedes...
Sure.
Per? Ole? How's it...
...coming?
Why are you... Why did you stop? We have to hurry! There's no time to...
Uh... Dig! Dig now, ya! Skroo Charles! Dig!
DIG, NO.
YA. NO. PAY PER AND OLE. THEN DIG. THEN SKROO, YA...

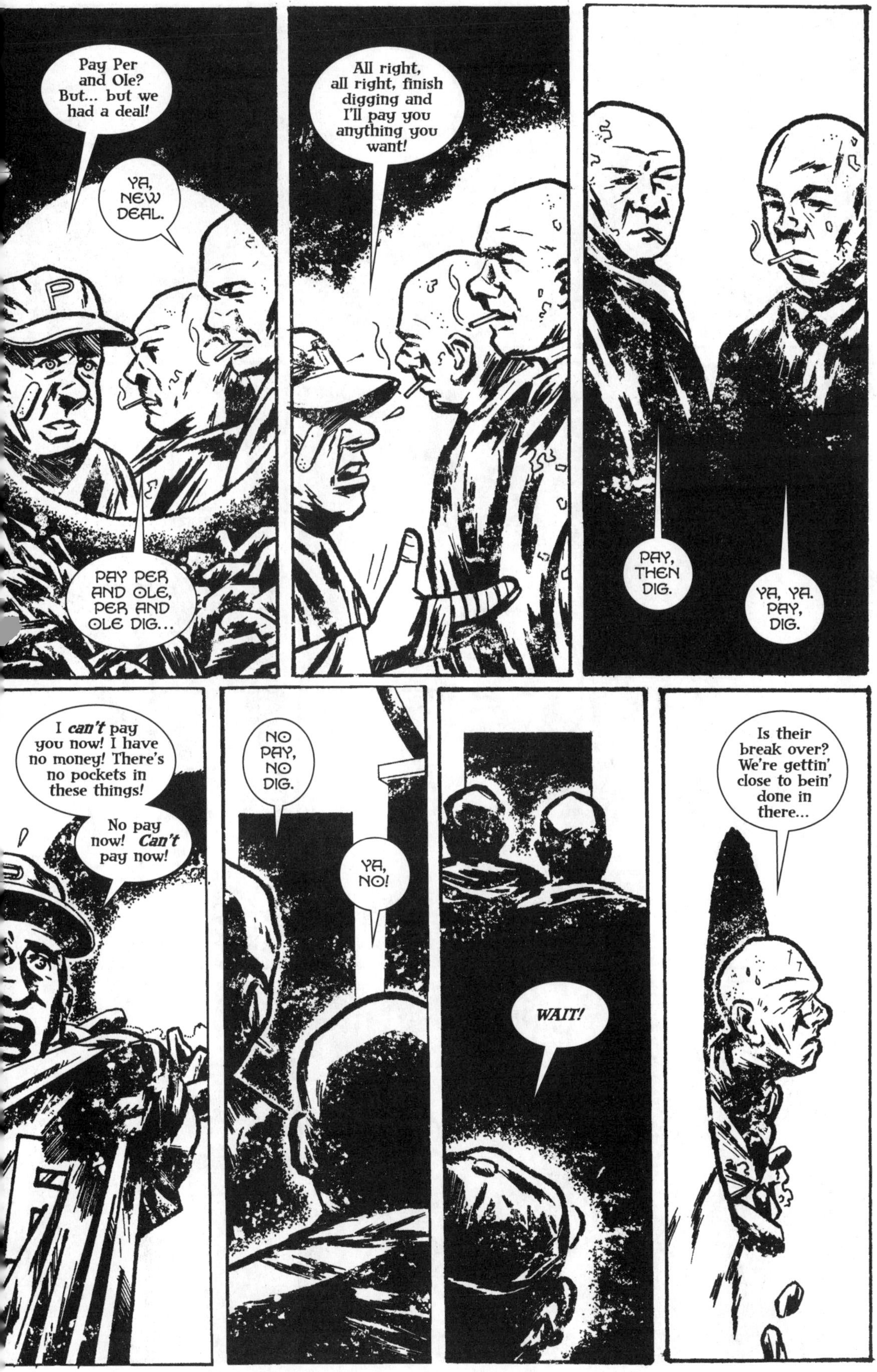
Pay Per and Ole? But... but we had a deal!
YA, NEW DEAL.
PAY PER AND OLE, PER AND OLE DIG...
All right, all right, finish digging and I'll pay you anything you want!
PAY, THEN DIG.
YA, YA. PAY, DIG.
I *can't* pay you now! I have no money! There's no pockets in these things!
No pay now! *Can't* pay now!
NO PAY, NO DIG.
YA, NO!
WAIT!
Is their break over? We're gettin' close to bein' done in there...

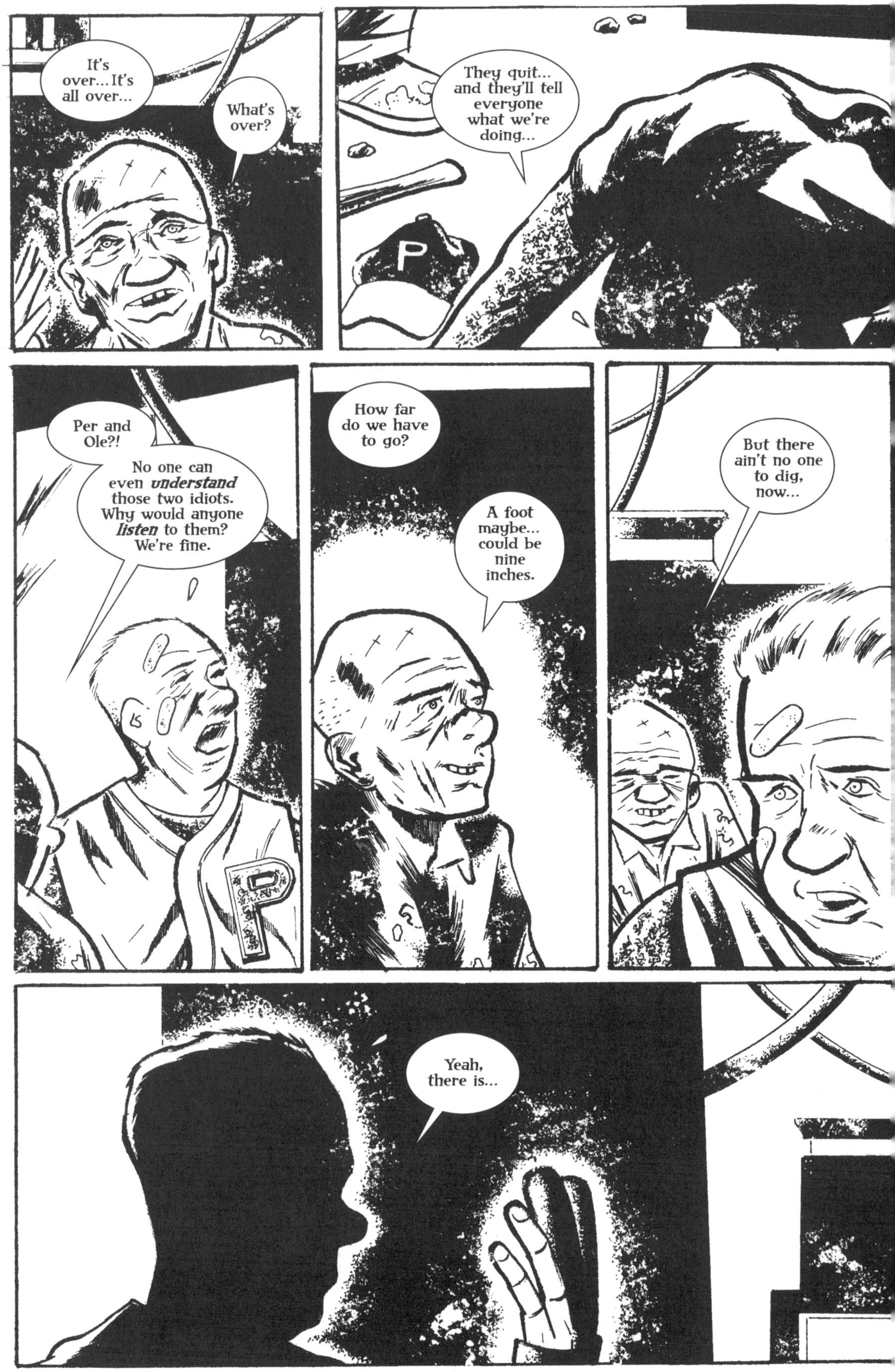
It's over...It's all over...
What's over?
They quit... and they'll tell everyone what we're doing...
Per and Ole?!
No one can even *understand* those two idiots. Why would anyone *listen* to them? We're fine.
How far do we have to go?
A foot maybe... could be nine inches.
But there ain't no one to dig, now...
Yeah, there is...

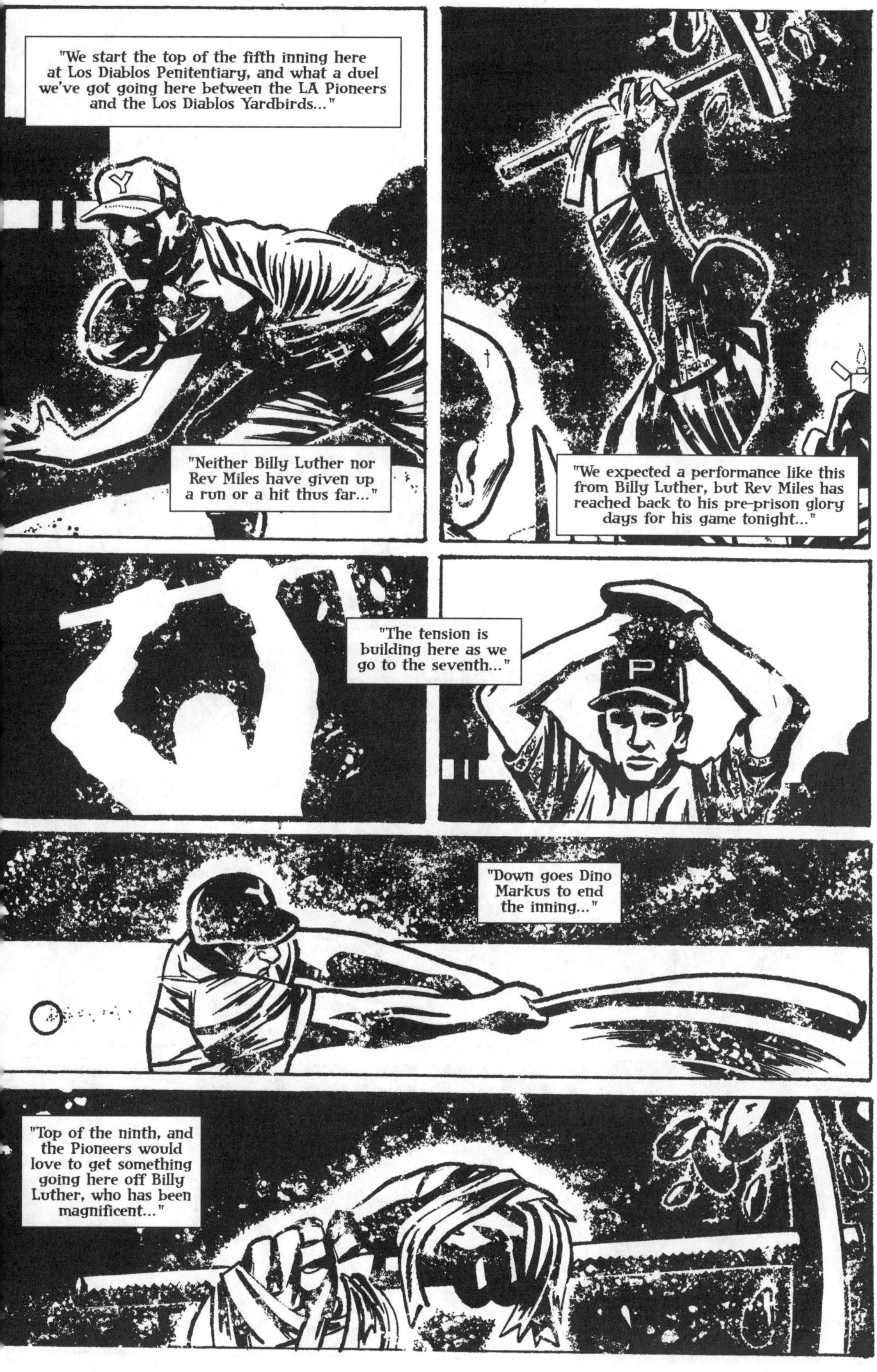
"We start the top of the fifth inning here at Los Diablos Penitentiary, and what a duel we've got going here between the LA Pioneers and the Los Diablos Yardbirds..."
"Neither Billy Luther nor Rev Miles have given up a run or a hit thus far..."
"We expected a performance like this from Billy Luther, but Rev Miles has reached back to his pre-prison glory days for his game tonight..."
"The tension is building here as we go to the seventh..."
"Down goes Dino Markus to end the inning..."
"Top of the ninth, and the Pioneers would love to get something going here off Billy Luther, who has been magnificent..."

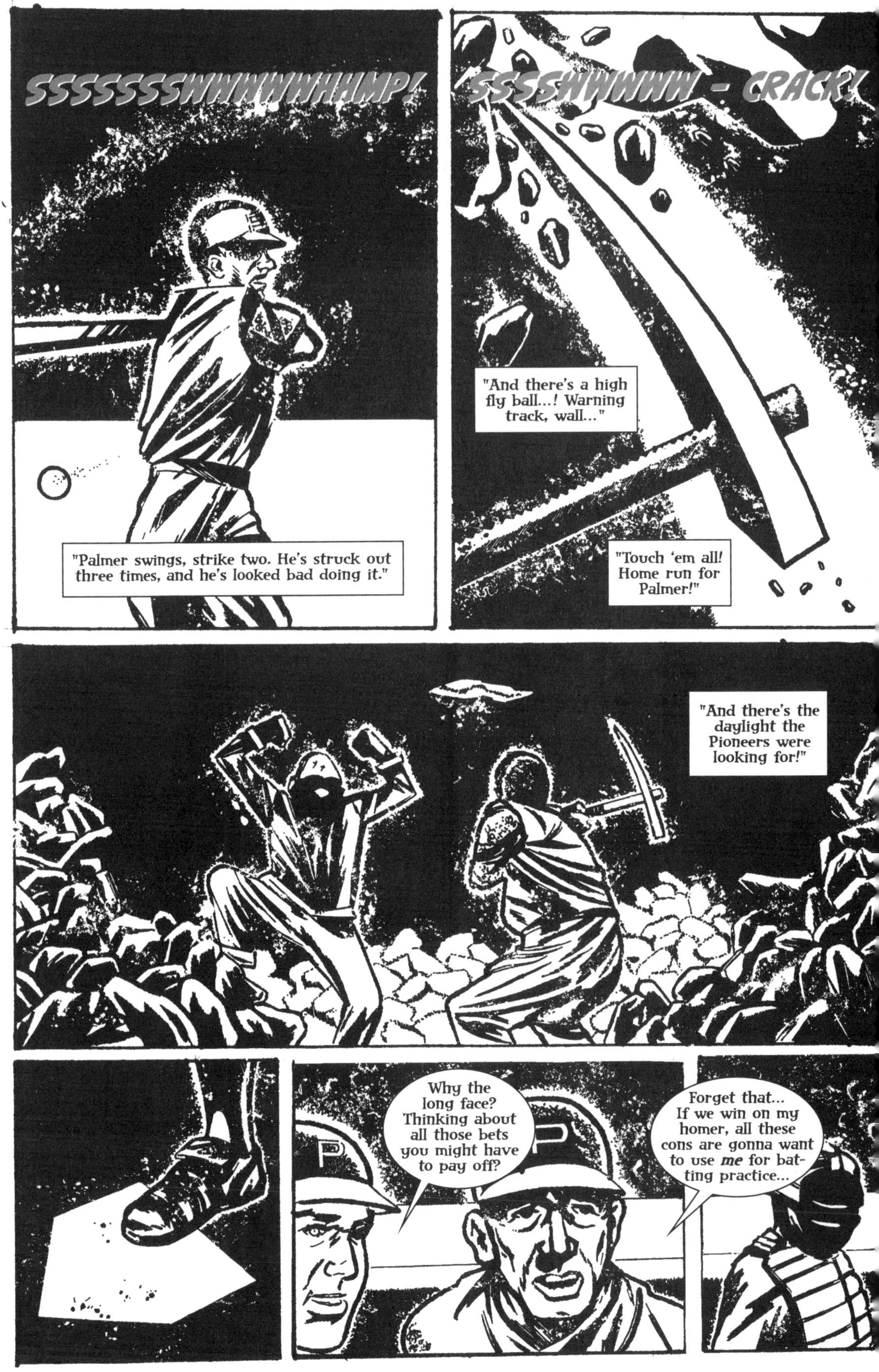
SSSSSSSWWWWWHHMP!
"Palmer swings, strike two. He's struck out three times, and he's looked bad doing it."
SSSSWWWWW - CRACK!
"And there's a high fly ball...! Warning track, wall..."
"Touch 'em all! Home run for Palmer!"
"And there's the daylight the Pioneers were looking for!"
Why the long face? Thinking about all those bets you might have to pay off?
Forget that... If we win on my homer, all these cons are gonna want to use *me* for batting practice...

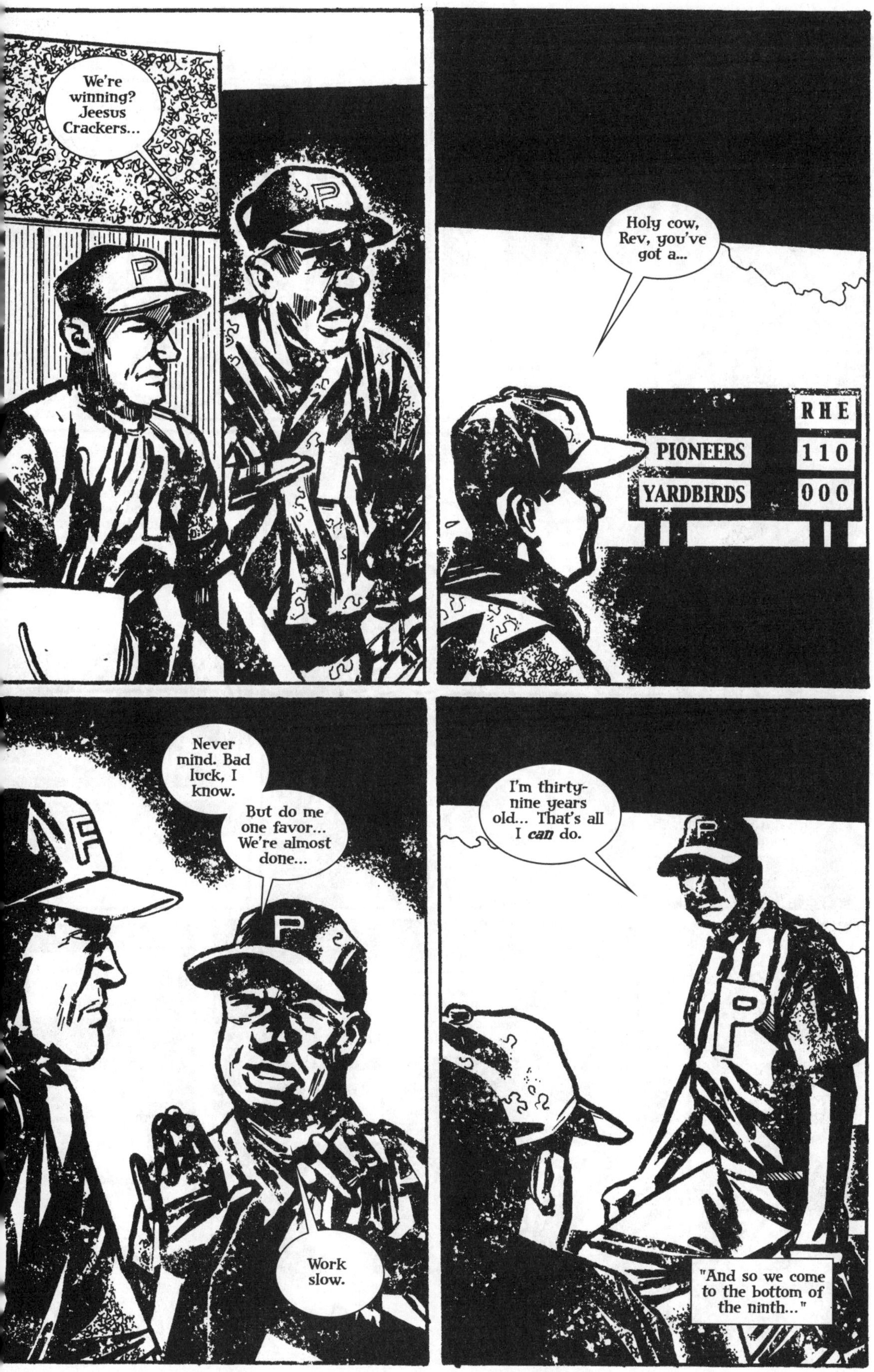
We're winning? Jeesus Crackers...
Holy cow, Rev, you've got a...
RHE
PIONEERS 110
YARDBIRDS 000
Never mind. Bad luck, I know.
But do me one favor... We're almost done...
Work slow.
I'm thirty-nine years old... That's all I *can* do.
"And so we come to the bottom of the ninth..."

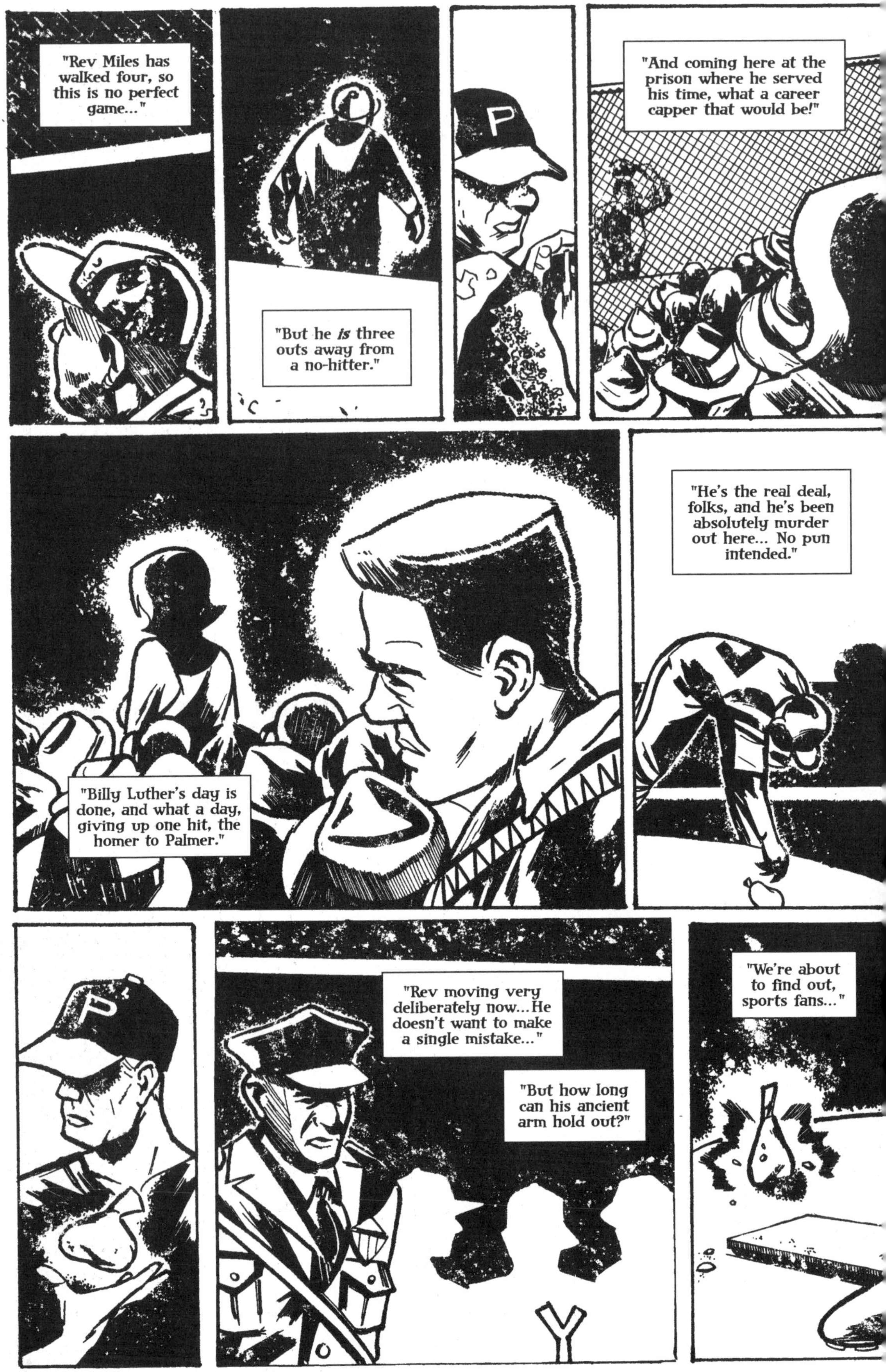
"Rev Miles has walked four, so this is no perfect game..."
"But he *is* three outs away from a no-hitter."
"And coming here at the prison where he served his time, what a career capper that would be!"
"Billy Luther's day is done, and what a day, giving up one hit, the homer to Palmer."
"He's the real deal, folks, and he's been absolutely murder out here... No pun intended."
"Rev moving very deliberately now...He doesn't want to make a single mistake..."
"But how long can his ancient arm hold out?"
"We're about to find out, sports fans..."

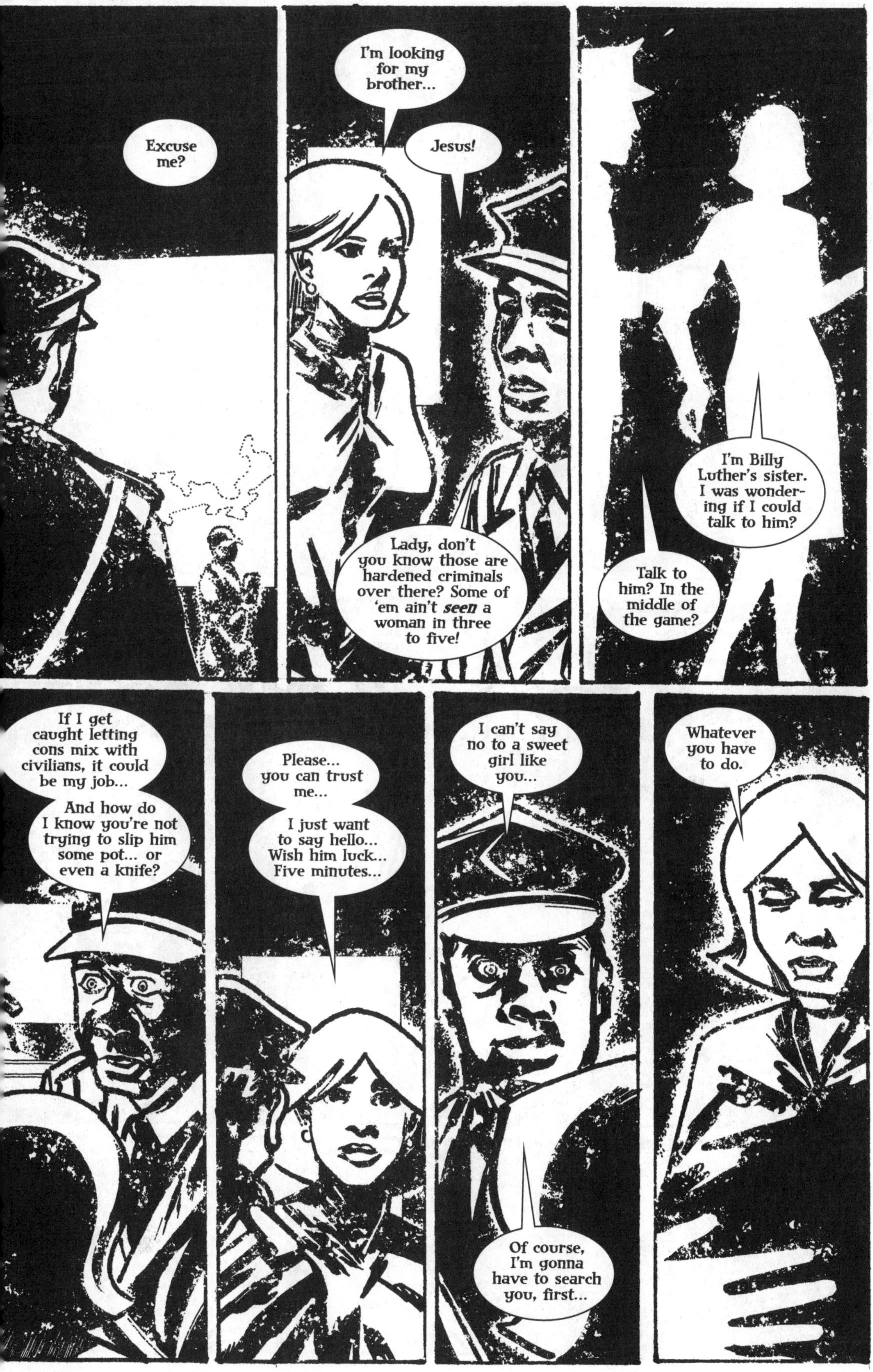

Excuse me?
I'm looking for my brother...
Jesus!
Lady, don't you know those are hardened criminals over there? Some of 'em ain't *seen* a woman in three to five!
I'm Billy Luther's sister. I was wondering if I could talk to him?
Talk to him? In the middle of the game?
If I get caught letting cons mix with civilians, it could be my job...
And how do I know you're not trying to slip him some pot... or even a knife?
Please... you can trust me...
I just want to say hello... Wish him luck... Five minutes...
I can't say no to a sweet girl like you...
Of course, I'm gonna have to search you, first...
Whatever you have to do.

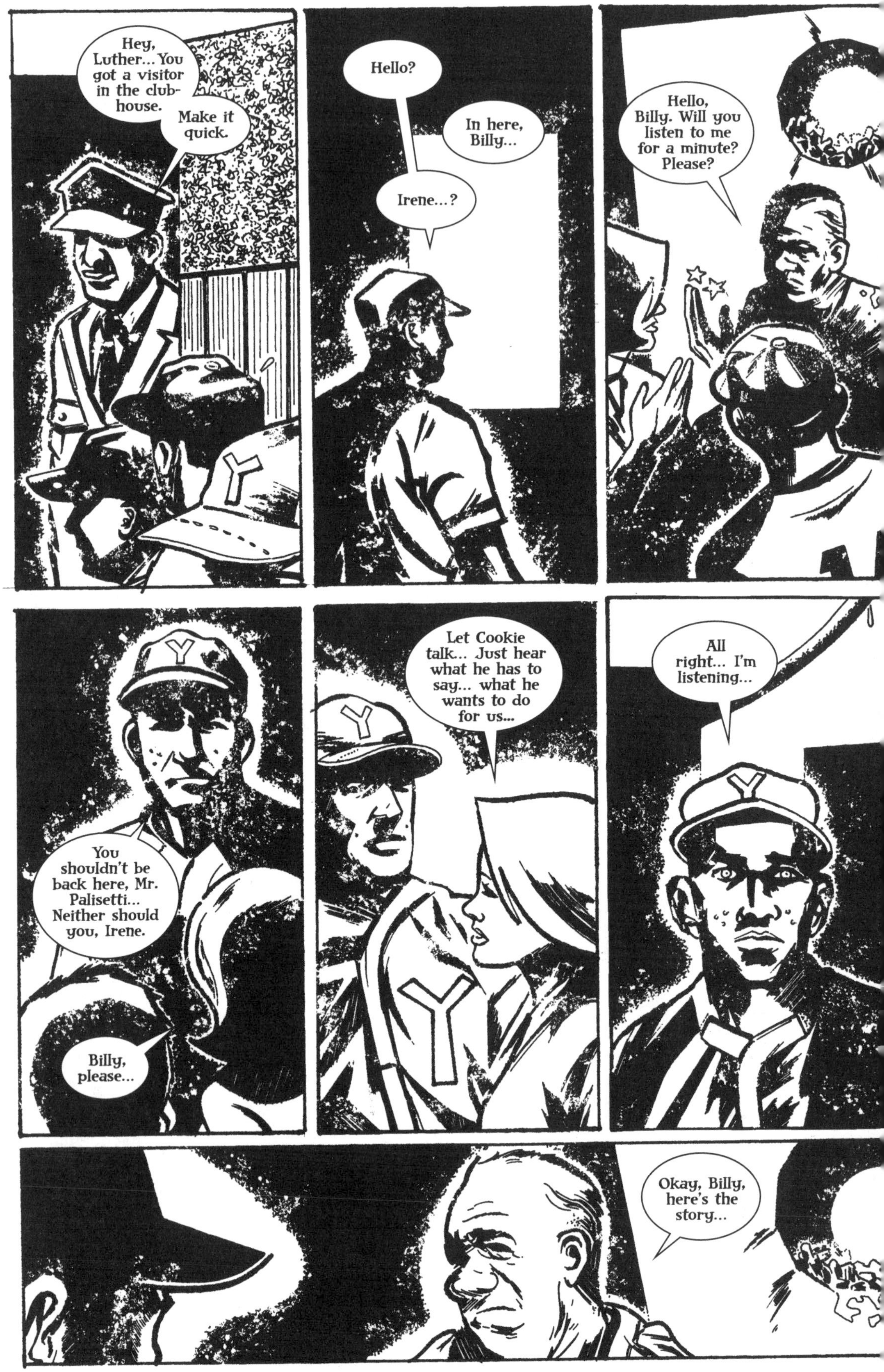
Hey, Luther... You got a visitor in the club-house.
Make it quick.
Hello?
Irene...?
In here, Billy...
Hello, Billy. Will you listen to me for a minute? Please?
You shouldn't be back here, Mr. Palisetti... Neither should you, Irene.
Billy, please...
Let Cookie talk... Just hear what he has to say... what he wants to do for us...
All right... I'm listening...
Okay, Billy, here's the story...

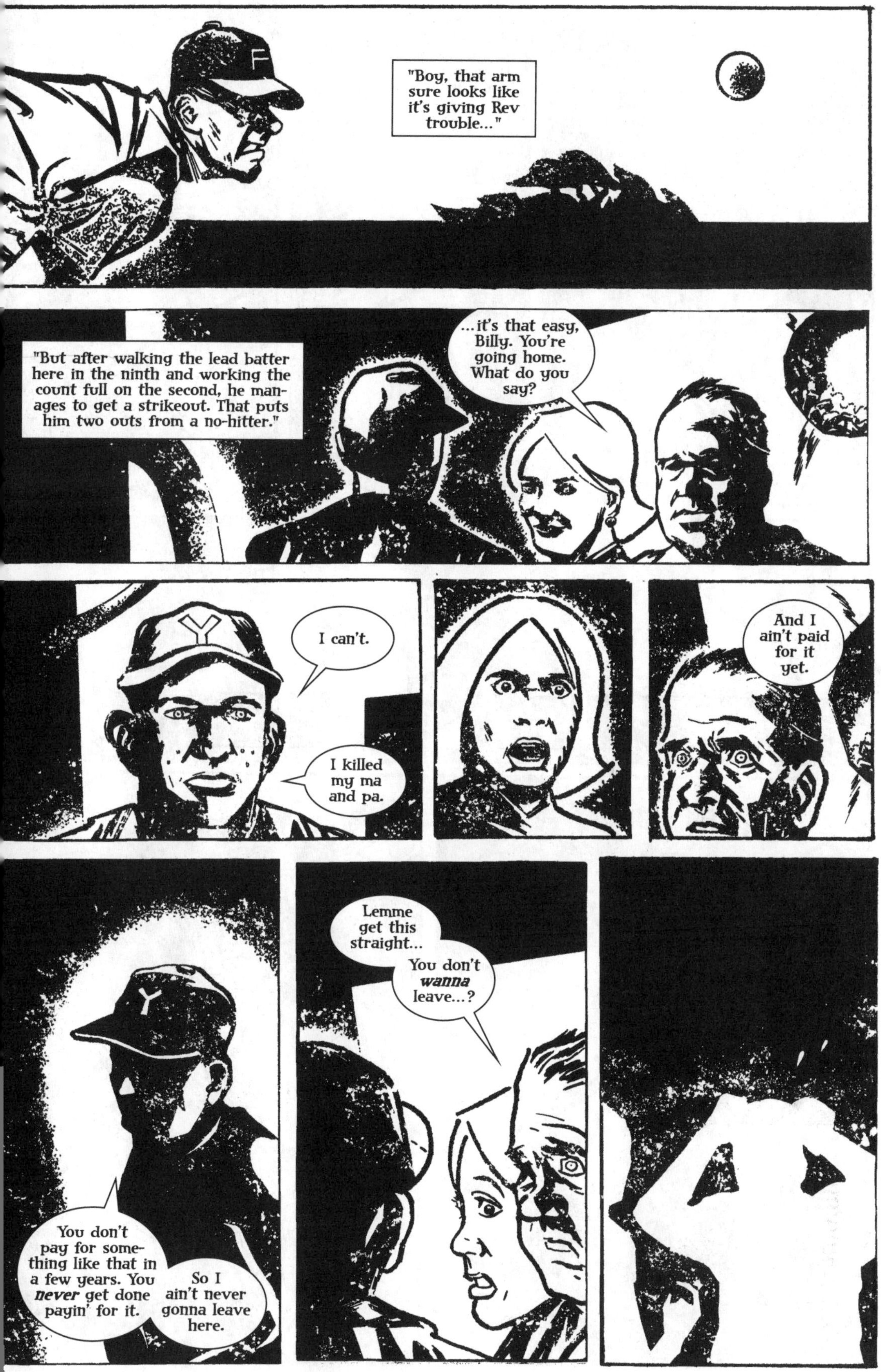
"Boy, that arm sure looks like it's giving Rev trouble..."
"But after walking the lead batter here in the ninth and working the count full on the second, he manages to get a strikeout. That puts him two outs from a no-hitter."
...it's that easy, Billy. You're going home. What do you say?
I can't.
I killed my ma and pa.
And I ain't paid for it yet.
You don't pay for something like that in a few years. You *never* get done payin' for it.
So I ain't never gonna leave here.
Lemme get this straight...
You don't *wanna* leave...?

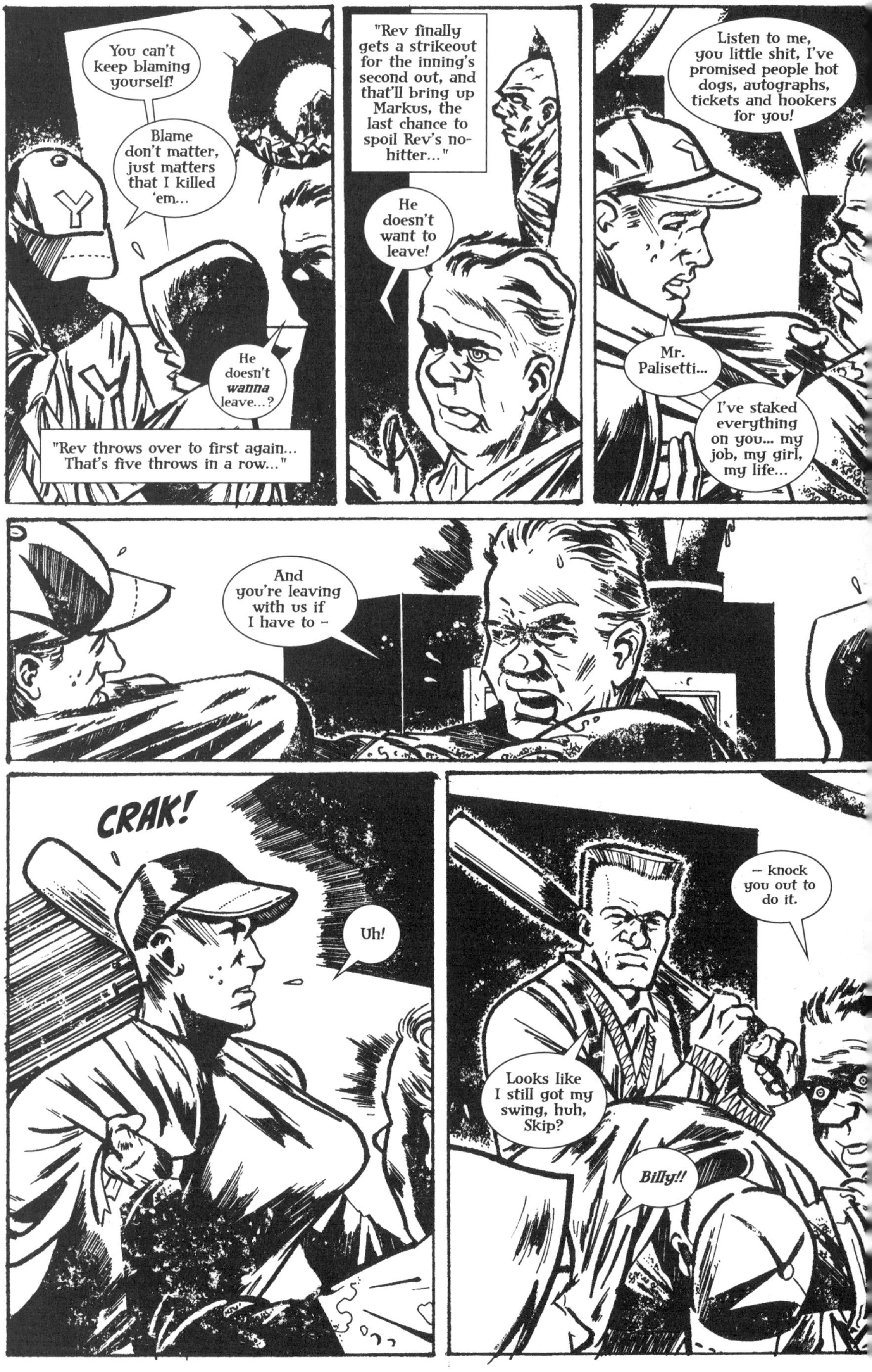
You can't keep blaming yourself!
Blame don't matter, just matters that I killed 'em...
He doesn't *wanna* leave...?
"Rev throws over to first again... That's five throws in a row..."
"Rev finally gets a strikeout for the inning's second out, and that'll bring up Markus, the last chance to spoil Rev's no-hitter..."
He doesn't want to leave!
Listen to me, you little shit, I've promised people hot dogs, autographs, tickets and hookers for you!
Mr. Palisetti...
I've staked everything on you... my job, my girl, my life...
And you're leaving with us if I have to –
CRAK!
Uh!
– knock you out to do it.
Looks like I still got my swing, huh, Skip?
Billy!!

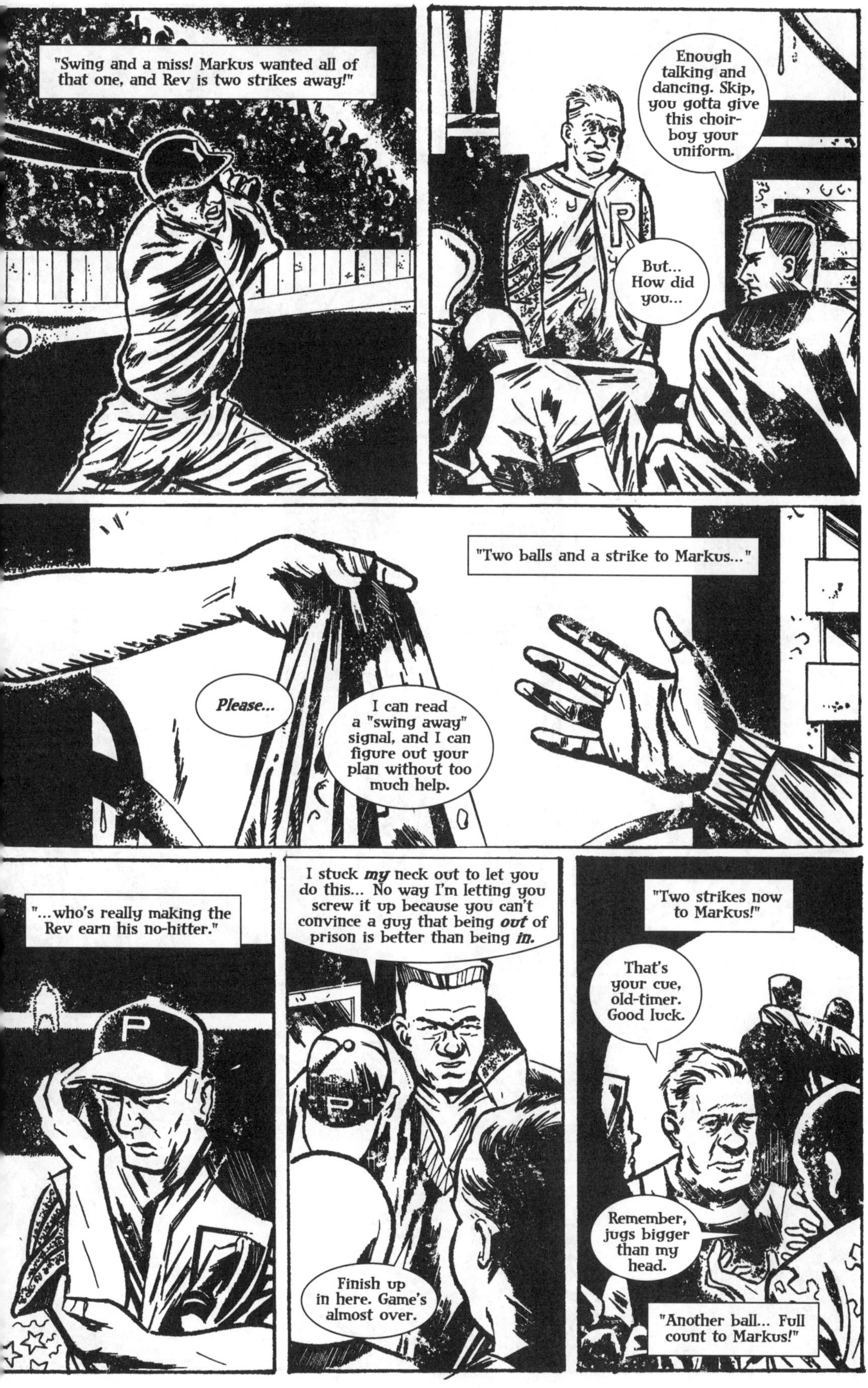

"Swing and a miss! Markus wanted all of that one, and Rev is two strikes away!"
Enough talking and dancing. Skip, you gotta give this choir-boy your uniform.
But... How did you...
"Two balls and a strike to Markus..."
Please...
I can read a "swing away" signal, and I can figure out your plan without too much help.
"...who's really making the Rev earn his no-hitter."
I stuck my neck out to let you do this... No way I'm letting you screw it up because you can't convince a guy that being out of prison is better than being in.
Finish up in here. Game's almost over.
"Two strikes now to Markus!"
That's your cue, old-timer. Good luck.
Remember, jugs bigger than my head.
"Another ball... Full count to Markus!"

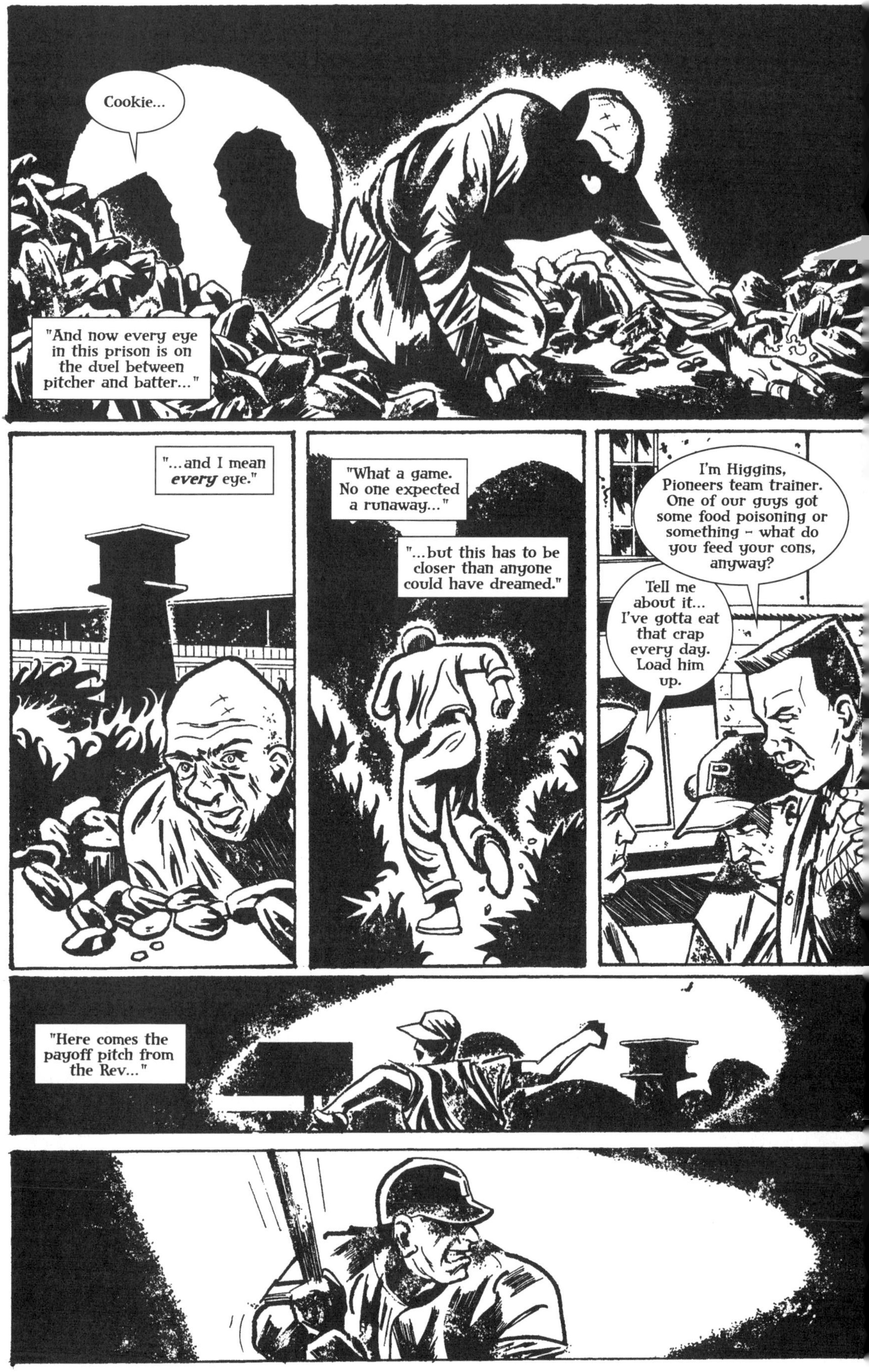
Cookie...
"And now every eye in this prison is on the duel between pitcher and batter..."
"...and I mean *every* eye."
"What a game. No one expected a runaway..."
"...but this has to be closer than anyone could have dreamed."
I'm Higgins, Pioneers team trainer. One of our guys got some food poisoning or something -- what do you feed your cons, anyway?
Tell me about it... I've gotta eat that crap every day. Load him up.
"Here comes the payoff pitch from the Rev..."

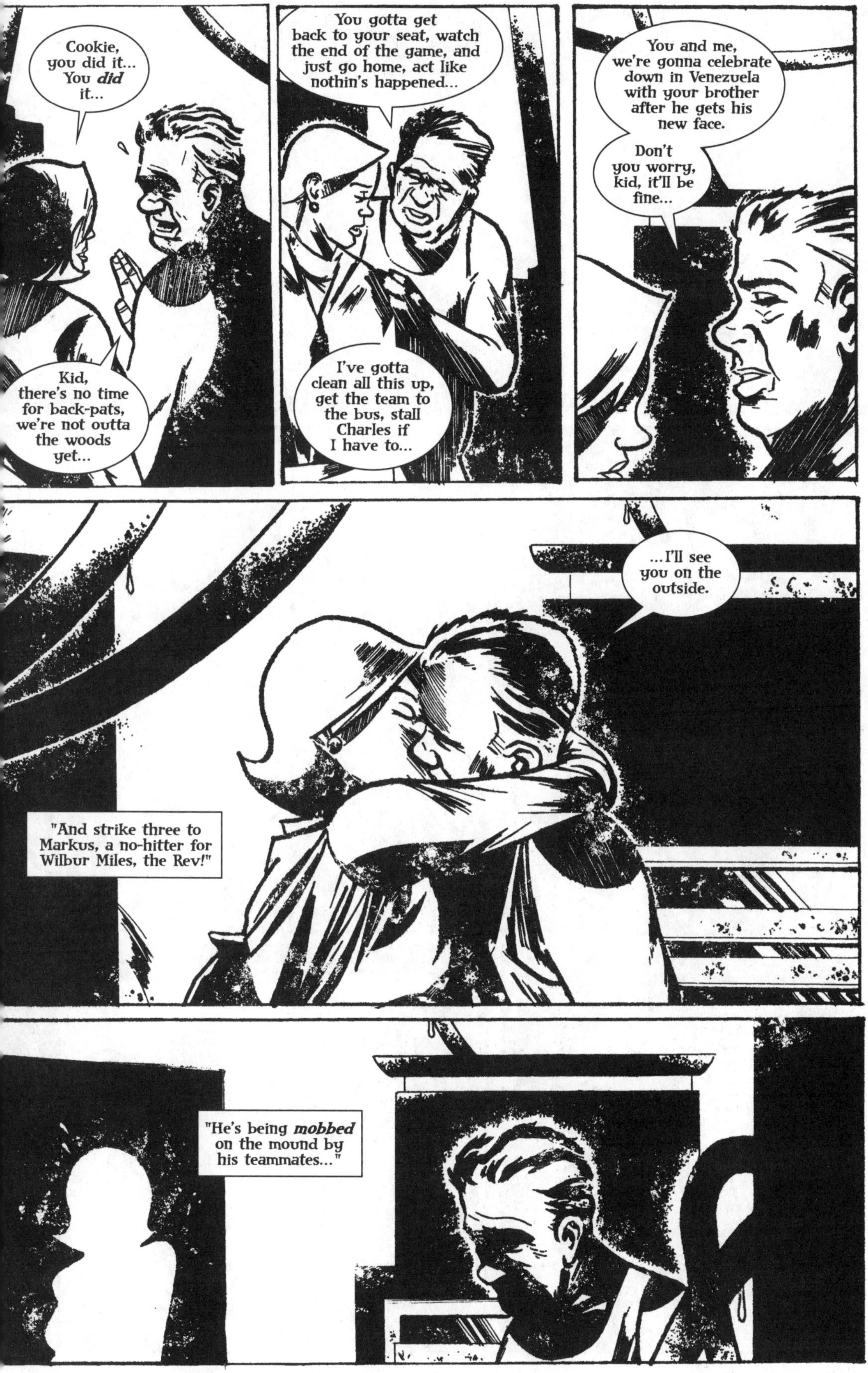
Cookie, you did it... You *did* it...
Kid, there's no time for back-pats, we're not outta the woods yet...
You gotta get back to your seat, watch the end of the game, and just go home, act like nothin's happened...
I've gotta clean all this up, get the team to the bus, stall Charles if I have to...
You and me, we're gonna celebrate down in Venezuela with your brother after he gets his new face.
Don't you worry, kid, it'll be fine...
...I'll see you on the outside.
"And strike three to Markus, a no-hitter for Wilbur Miles, the Rev!"
"He's being *mobbed* on the mound by his teammates..."

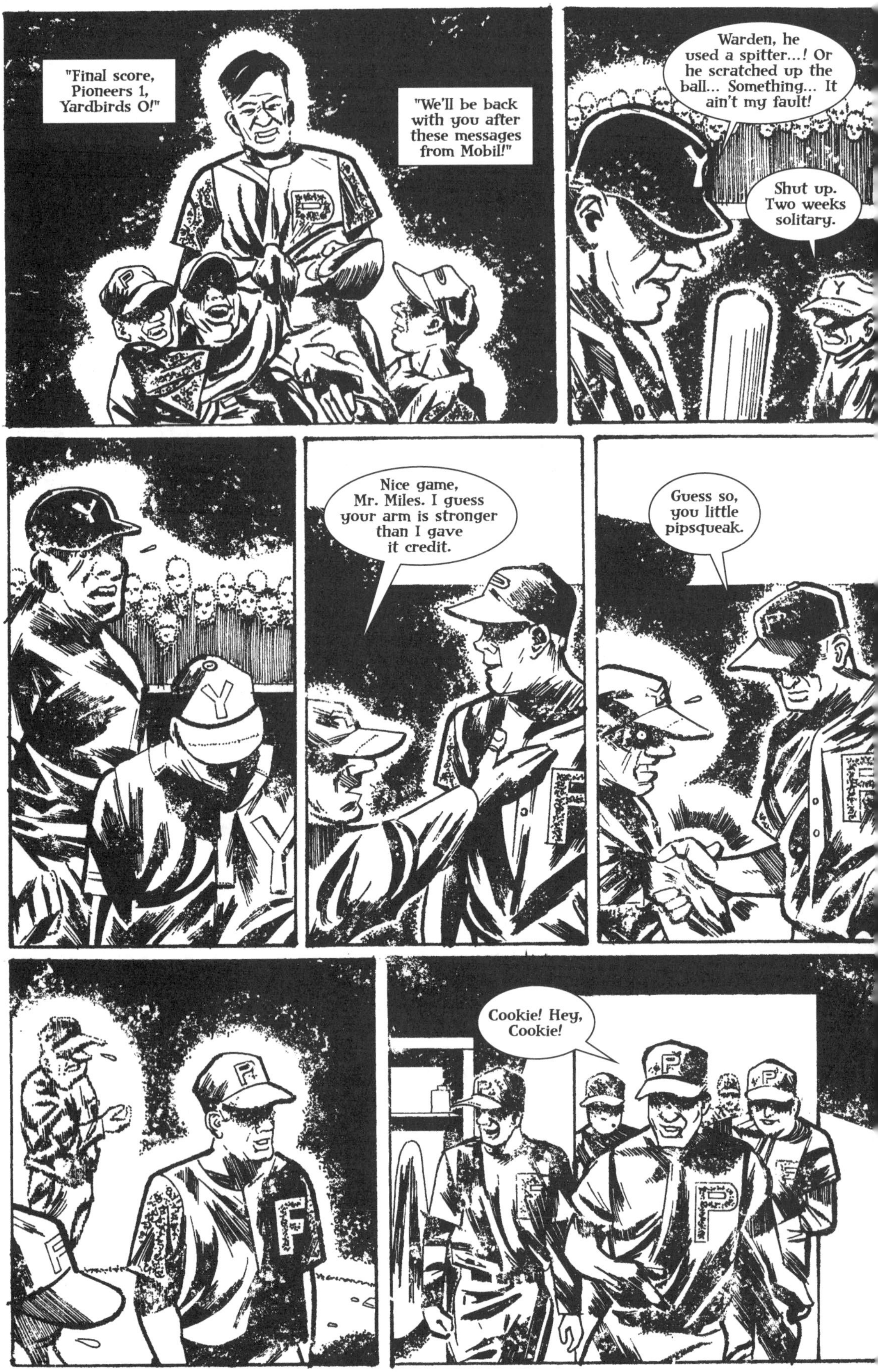
"Final score, Pioneers 1, Yardbirds O!"
"We'll be back with you after these messages from Mobil!"
Warden, he used a spitter...! Or he scratched up the ball... Something... It ain't my fault!
Shut up. Two weeks solitary.
Nice game, Mr. Miles. I guess your arm is stronger than I gave it credit.
Guess so, you little pipsqueak.
Cookie! Hey, Cookie!

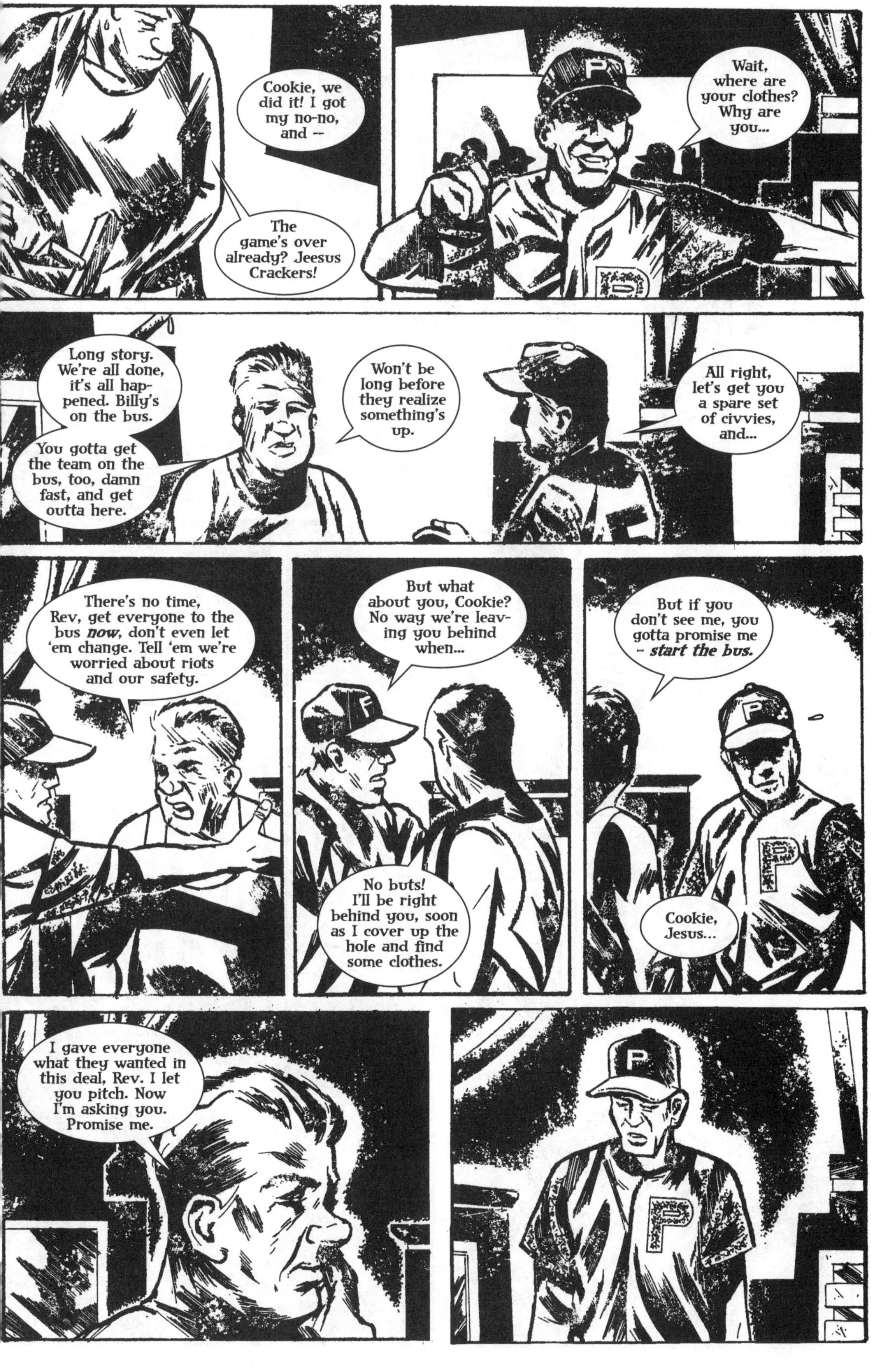
Cookie, we did it! I got my no-no, and --
The game's over already? Jeesus Crackers!
Wait, where are your clothes? Why are you...
Long story. We're all done, it's all hap-pened. Billy's on the bus.
You gotta get the team on the bus, too, damn fast, and get outta here.
Won't be long before they realize something's up.
All right, let's get you a spare set of civvies, and...
There's no time, Rev, get everyone to the bus *now*, don't even let 'em change. Tell 'em we're worried about riots and our safety.
But what about you, Cookie? No way we're leav-ing you behind when...
No buts! I'll be right behind you, soon as I cover up the hole and find some clothes.
But if you don't see me, you gotta promise me - ***start the bus.***
Cookie, Jesus...
I gave everyone what they wanted in this deal, Rev. I let you pitch. Now I'm asking you. Promise me.

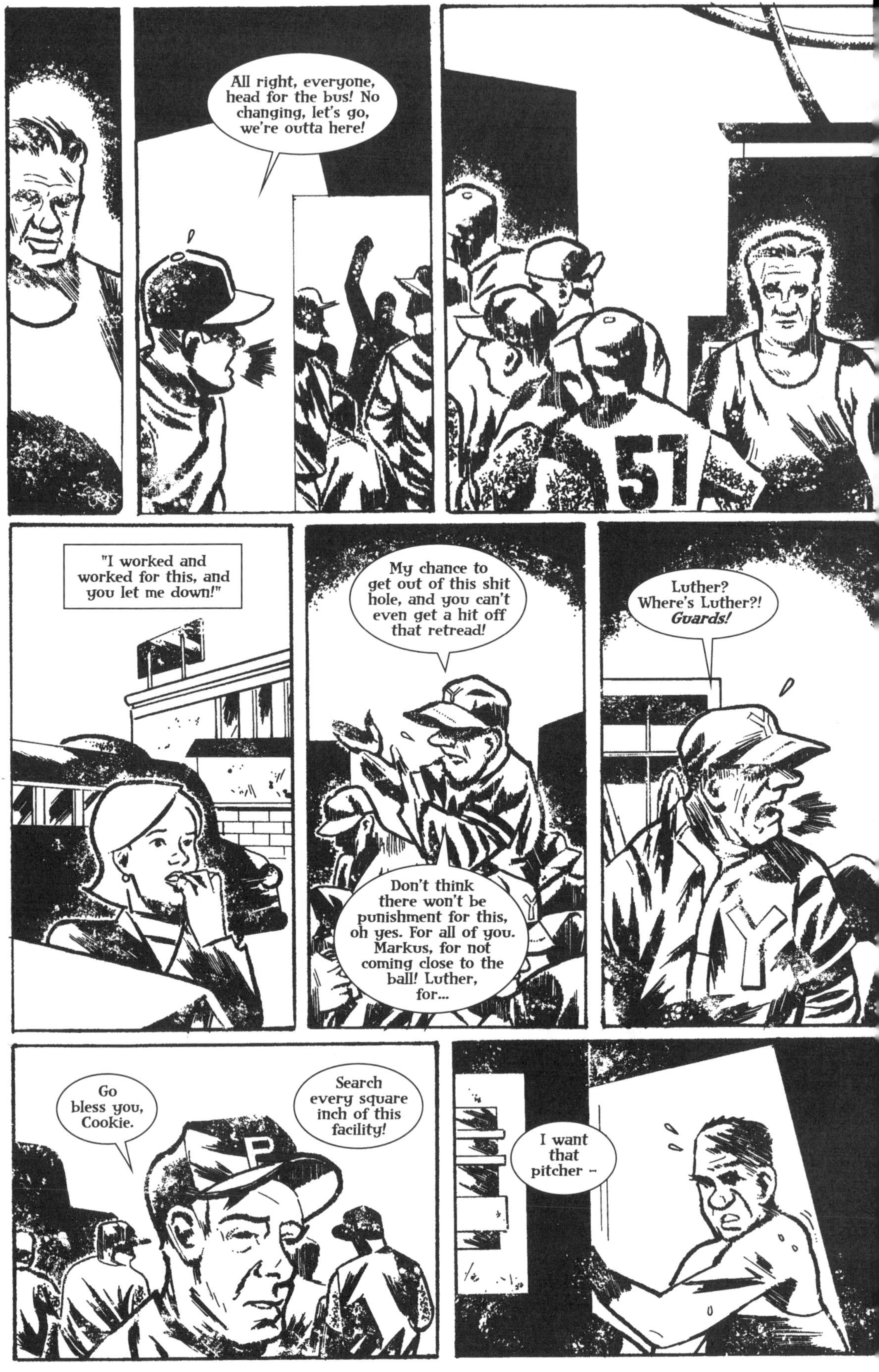
All right, everyone, head for the bus! No changing, let's go, we're outta here!
57
"I worked and worked for this, and you let me down!"
My chance to get out of this shit hole, and you can't even get a hit off that retread!
Don't think there won't be punishment for this, oh yes. For all of you. Markus, for not coming close to the ball! Luther, for...
Luther? Where's Luther?! *Guards!*
Go bless you, Cookie.
Search every square inch of this facility!
I want that pitcher –

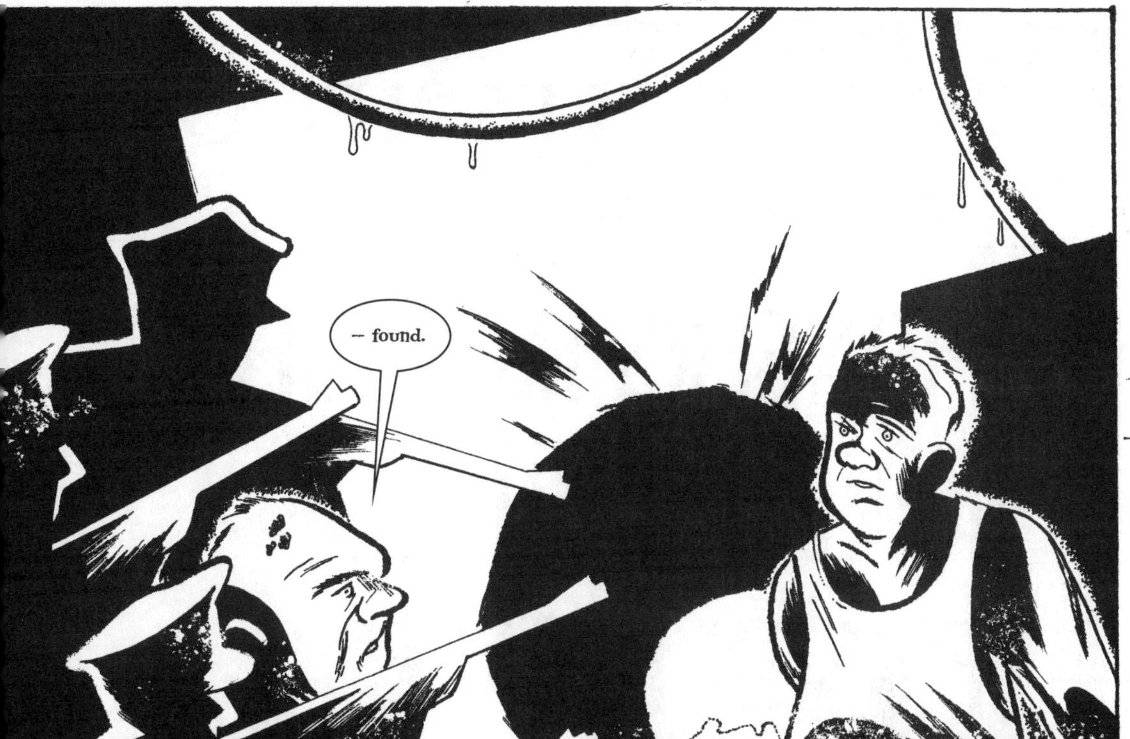
– found.

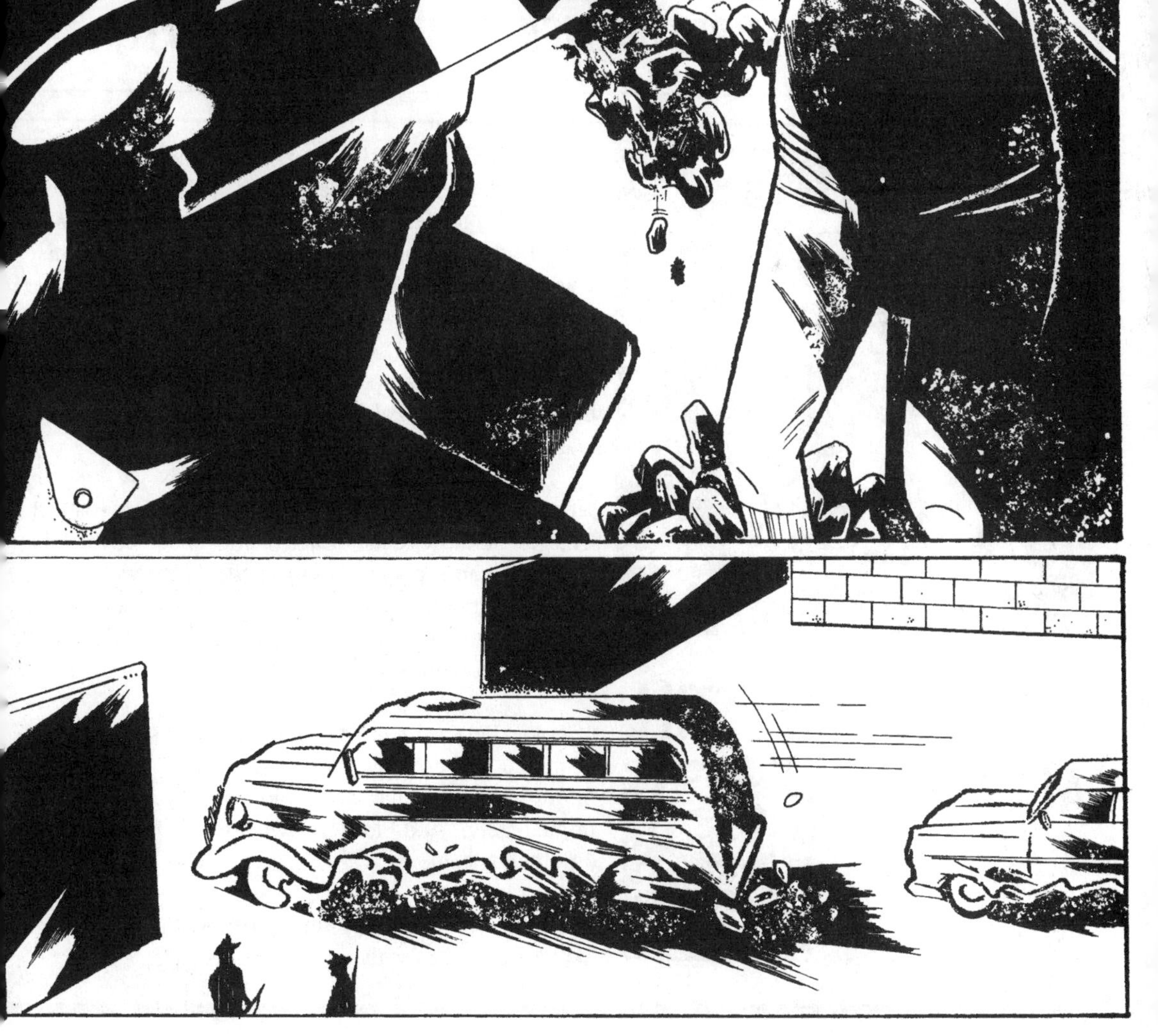

LOS ANGELES RECORD

PIONEERS MANAGER ARRESTED IN PRISON ESCAPE

STAR PITCHER ESCAPES THROUGH TUNNEL, AIDED BY SKIPPER

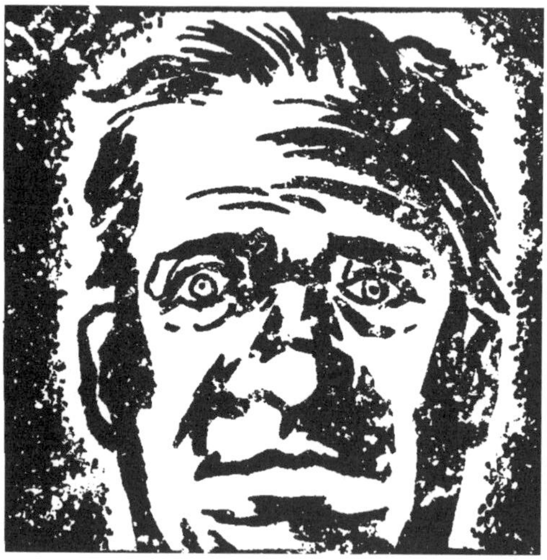

Authorities arrested Los Angeles Pioneers Manager Cookie Palisetti yesterday, after Palisetti allegedly engineered the escape of onetime Pioneers prospect Billy Luther through a tunnel under Los Diablos State Prison. As today's edition went to press, Luther remained at large.

When told the escape scheme was unprecedented in baseball history, Palisetti's only comment was, "At least I made my mark on the game."

"It's an outrage," said Los Diablos Warden Elswick Charles of the events, which came under cover of a goodwill game played between the Pioneers and the prison's champion squad, the Yardbirds. "In addition to being blatantly illegal, it demeans the spirit of the game and certainly taints their victory."

"Cookie Palisetti has been relieved of his managerial post, and will be replaced by Wilbur (Rev) Miles, one of our most popular and beloved players, effective immediately," said Pioneers owner Oscar Blakemore in a written statement.

Billy Luther had already served the first three years of his life sentence for the murder of his parents in

OTHER ESCAPEE STILL AT LARGE

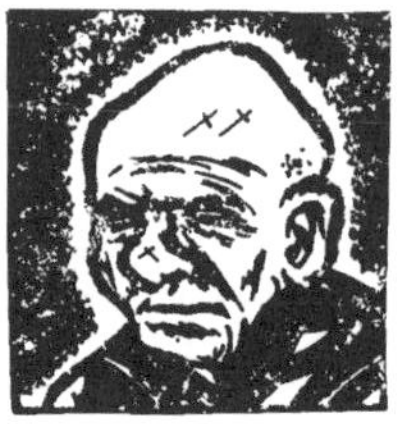

Inmate Stevens, also known as "Lorem Ipsum," dolor sit amet, consectatuer adipiscing elit. Sed mollis sern sit arnet leo. Praesent condimentum, nibh in malesuada

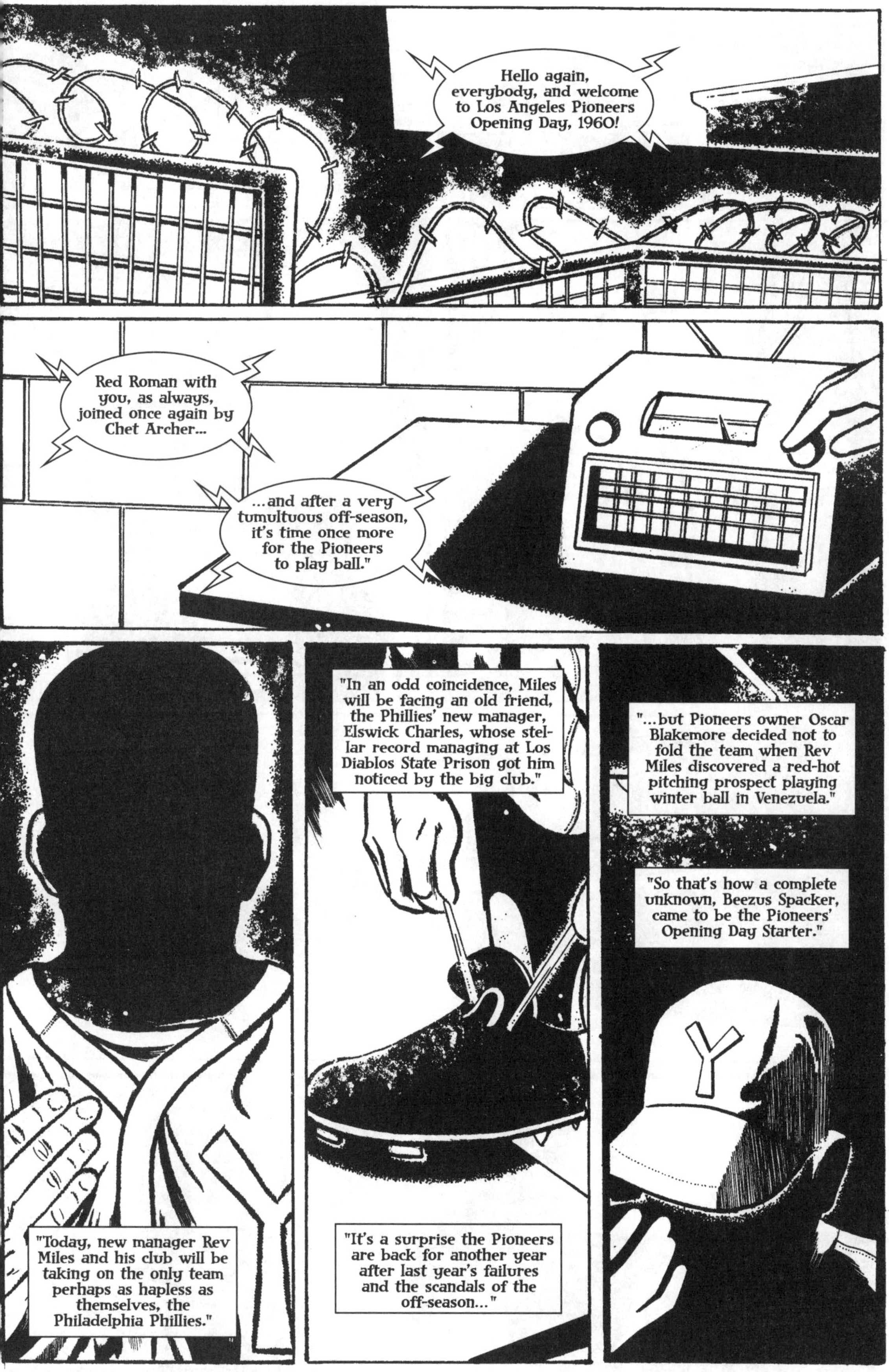
Hello again, everybody, and welcome to Los Angeles Pioneers Opening Day, 1960!
Red Roman with you, as always, joined once again by Chet Archer...
...and after a very tumultuous off-season, it's time once more for the Pioneers to play ball."
"Today, new manager Rev Miles and his club will be taking on the only team perhaps as hapless as themselves, the Philadelphia Phillies."
"In an odd coincidence, Miles will be facing an old friend, the Phillies' new manager, Elswick Charles, whose stellar record managing at Los Diablos State Prison got him noticed by the big club."
"It's a surprise the Pioneers are back for another year after last year's failures and the scandals of the off-season..."
"...but Pioneers owner Oscar Blakemore decided not to fold the team when Rev Miles discovered a red-hot pitching prospect playing winter ball in Venezuela."
"So that's how a complete unknown, Beezus Spacker, came to be the Pioneers' Opening Day Starter."

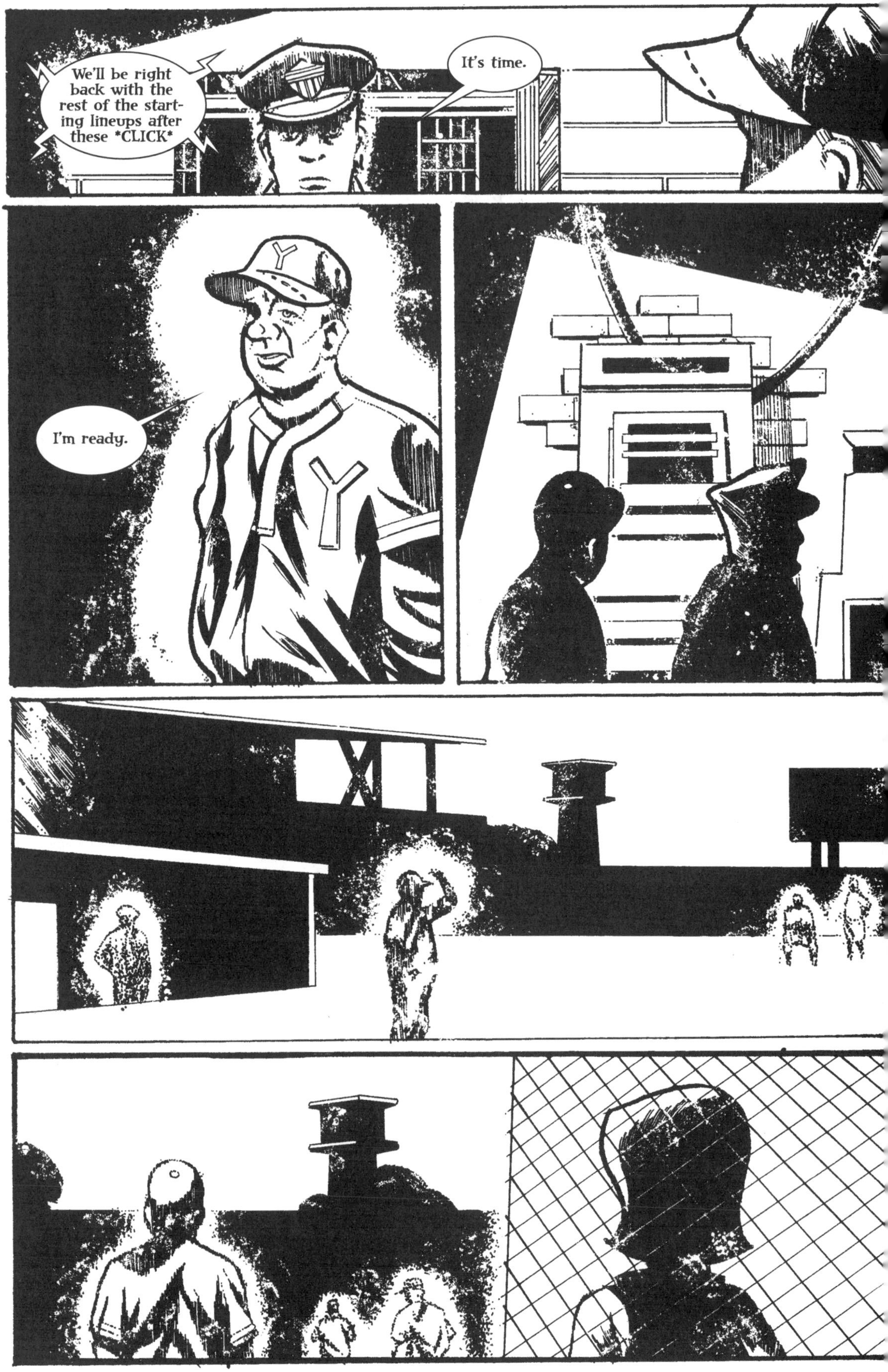
We'll be right back with the rest of the starting lineups after these *CLICK*
It's time.
I'm ready.

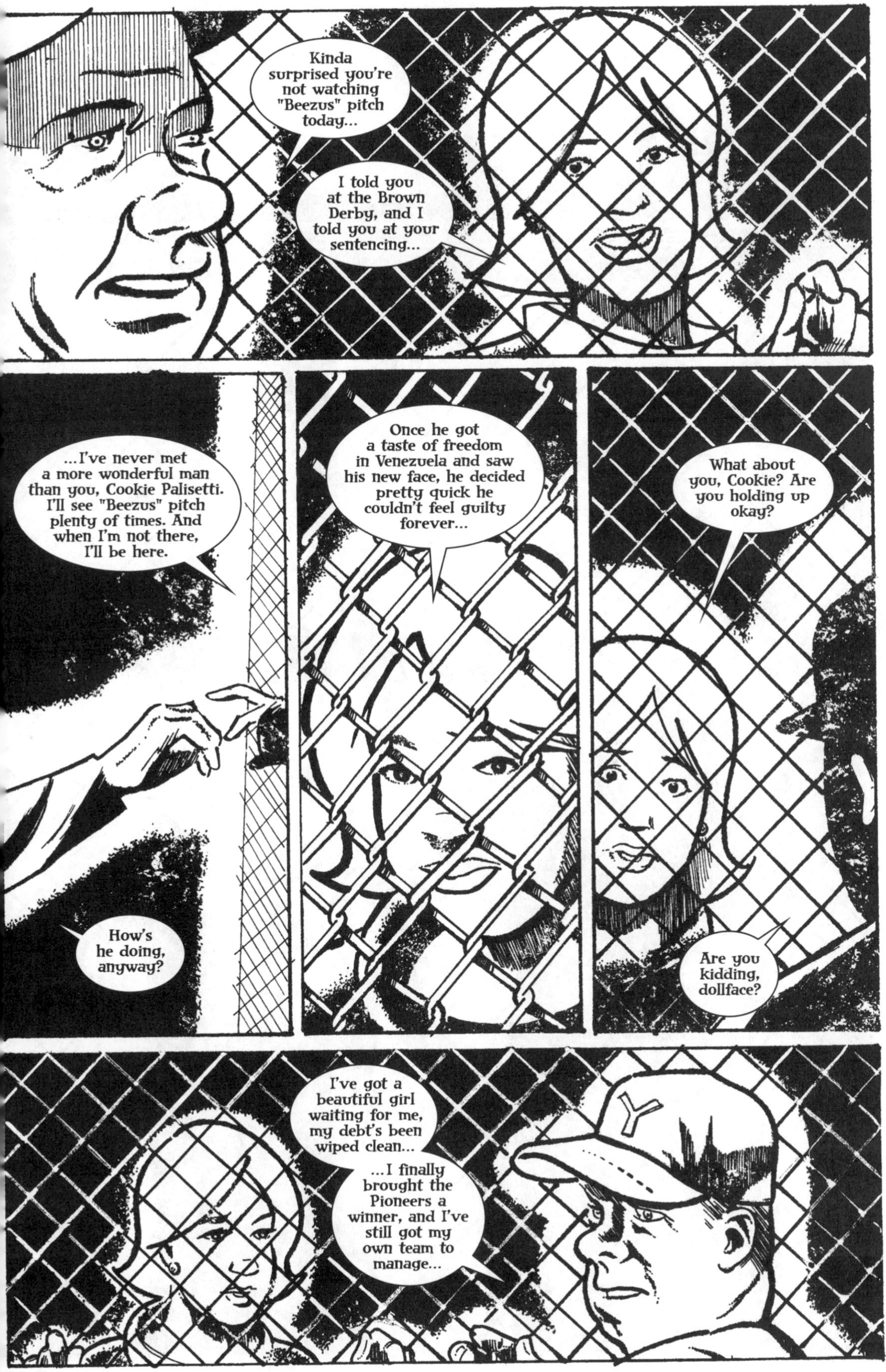

Kinda surprised you're not watching "Beezus" pitch today...
I told you at the Brown Derby, and I told you at your sentencing...
...I've never met a more wonderful man than you, Cookie Palisetti. I'll see "Beezus" pitch plenty of times. And when I'm not there, I'll be here.
How's he doing, anyway?
Once he got a taste of freedom in Venezuela and saw his new face, he decided pretty quick he couldn't feel guilty forever...
What about you, Cookie? Are you holding up okay?
Are you kidding, dollface?
I've got a beautiful girl waiting for me, my debt's been wiped clean...
...I finally brought the Pioneers a winner, and I've still got my own team to manage...

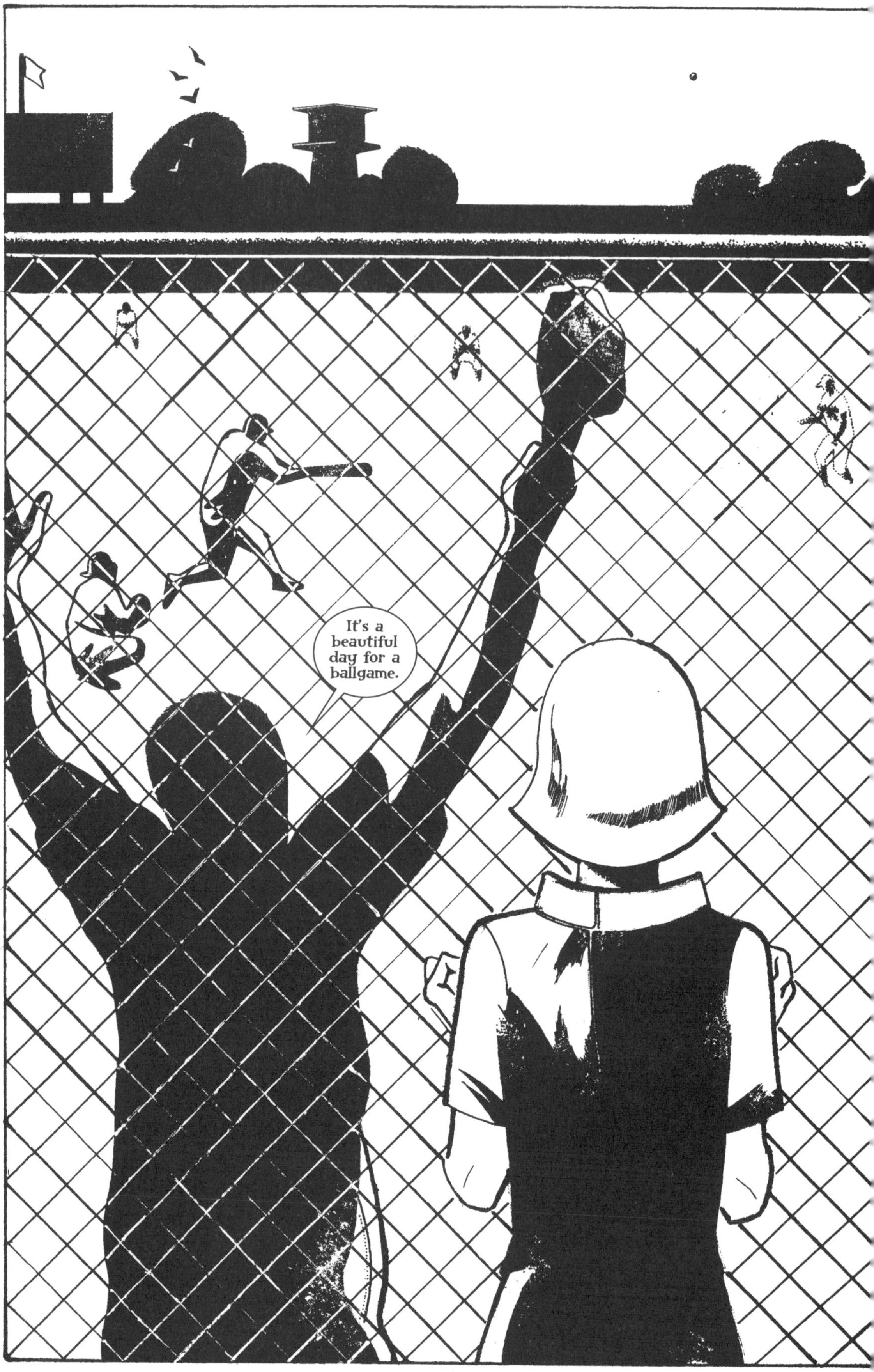
It's a beautiful day for a ballgame.

END